TEMPLE BETH-EL

ROCHESTER, N.Y.

139 WINTON RD. S.

והגית
בו
יומם
ולילה

BERMAN

MW00570492

CHATTERING MAN

CHATTERING MAN

Stories and a Novella

MERRILL JOAN GERBER

LONGSTREET PRESS
Atlanta, Georgia

Published by
LONGSTREET PRESS, INC.
2150 Newmarket Parkway
Suite 102
Marietta, Georgia 30067

Printed in the United States of America

1st printing, 1991

Library of Congress Catalog Number: 91-61930

ISBN 1-56352-011-7

This book was printed by R. R. Donnelly & Sons, Harrisonburg,
Virginia. The text was set in Bodoni by Coghill Book Typesetting,
Richmond, Virginia. Book design by Jill Dible.

Cover photo by Joe Felzman, courtesy of Paula Cooper Gallery, New
York. Sculpture by Jonathan Borofsky.

For
Cynthia Ozick

/

ACKNOWLEDGMENTS

"Chicken Skin Sandwiches," winner of the Readers' Choice Award from *Prairie Schooner*, first appeared in that magazine.

"Honest Mistakes" first appeared in *McCall's*.

"Hairdos," winner of the *Fiction Network* contest, first appeared in that publication. It also appeared, in slightly altered form, in *Seventeen*.

"A View of Boston Commons" first appeared in *Belles Lettres*.

"Rescue" and "The Leaf Lady" first appeared in *Crosscurrents*.

"Mozart You Can't Give Them" and "Comes an Earthquake" first appeared in *Sewanee Review*.

"The Blood Pressure Bunch and the Alzheimer's Gang" first appeared in *Amelia*.

"Starry Night" first appeared in *Wascana Review*.

"The Next Meal Is *Lunch*" first appeared in *Phoebe: A SUNY Women's Studies Journal*.

CONTENTS

I

....

CHATTERING
MAN

. . . .

In the days I was living in a rickety co-op in Berkeley with
a young man named Ben, my mother—instead of writing
me letters—used to send me photocopies which she made in
gay colors on the cartridge copier my father had bought for
his office. One day she enclosed in a large brown envelope a
mammogram, which I assumed was of one of my father's
patients. The breast was quite small—little roads and by-
ways crisscrossed within it, unlabeled, like a primitive map
of some new land. Just the one breast had a lonely, lost
quality to it, outlined as it was in blue ink on white paper.
My mother had drawn a box around a little cluster in the
breast where many of the lines intersected; it might have
been a small town. She had written in the margin, using an
orange marker pen: "Man's Fate."

I walked over to Ben's desk and dropped the picture next
to his shopping list. He was kitchen manager of the co-op
that semester and was busy ordering food for the week's
meals. He had written so far:

> 100 lbs broccoli
> 50 dozen eggs
> 200 gals milk
> 75 chickens, cut up
> 2 pounds chocolate chips
> 30 lbs halvah

He reached behind his chair and pressed my leg, just under my knee, with the outer part of his wrist. He always did this, to avoid having to look up from his work, while at the same time giving me a little of the attention I craved. I was always needing his attention. And I was deeply comforted that Ben was in charge of food. As his roommate, I felt I would have special privileges if an emergency occurred—though I had never asked him to compromise himself.

He handed the mammogram back to me. I carried it over to the wall above my bed and taped it up with the other items my mother had recently sent me—the actual knot of my umbilicus (I called it my bellybutton), a poisonous oleander leaf, an article from *Time* about the discovery of Anne Frank's family photograph album, and an article on the sexual harassment of female students by professors. This last was probably sent in response to my mentioning to her in a letter that when I'd baby-sat for my psych professor's son, I'd ended up spending the night at the house. I'd told my mother that my professor had come home very late from a date and, finding me asleep on the couch, decided not to wake me. I wrote her that I'd slept there till the morning and then had breakfast with him and his three-year-old son. It was my way of letting my mother know that I was not spending every single night in my own bed. She didn't know I was living with Ben. She thought my roommate was an Orthodox Jewish girl named Sylvia Cohen. My mother was convinced that Sylvia Cohen would be very good for me; she thought that if I lived with Sylvia Cohen long enough I might come to my senses and decide to spend my "junior year abroad" in Israel instead of in Austria. For several weeks I had had actual and absolute visceral knowledge that I wanted to spend my junior year in bed with Ben, but I was afraid to tell this to my mother. My parents had already sent the overseas office a deposit, refundable till mid-May, and even after that with a note from a school psychologist.

4

In that period of my life I'd been having a recurring dream about my mother: in it she was strapped to a chair in our backyard and a masked bandit was boring a hole in her head with a drill. He wasn't using an electric drill, but a red-handled device shaped like an old-fashioned eggbeater. While he held the wooden handle, he slowly turned a little metal wheel which meshed with another gear which made the drill bit bite into my mother's skull.

After I had had the dream three times in one week, I called my older sister Cleo at Yale, where she was in graduate school. I told her about the dream; since we'd shared a room as children, we'd always told each other our dreams. Over the phone I recited every detail. I confessed I thought the dream meant I wanted my mother to die.

"That's my dream, Annie, so don't worry!" she said. "You don't have to feel guilty."

"How can it be your dream? I just dreamed it last night!"

"I had it last year and told *you* about it! You stole it from me."

"That's impossible. It has to be my dream. I had it in my own brain. I can actually see the bandit right this second, the shape of his head in his knitted ski mask, the way he's leaning over her, the sound of the drill as he hits Mommy's skull bone."

"That's because I told it to you that way," Cleo said.

"I already put it in my dream book," I said.

"It's in mine, too," Cleo said.

"Well, our biographers will have to figure it out," I said. We always joked about our respective biographers, but we both knew only Cleo would be famous some day. "But, Cleo," I said, "one more thing before we hang up. What do you think is more important, love or Europe?"

"You learn a lot from love," Cleo said, "but Europe is bigger."

"Are you asleep, Ben?" I asked. His head had been down flat on his desk for some time, over the shopping list. "I hope we can go out for dinner soon. I would sell my body for mu-shu pork this instant." I added, "I'll pay—I know you have no money left this week."

Ben lifted his head and added an item to his list. "What about your paper?" he asked. Because he was older, he thought it was his duty to act as my conscience.

"Monosodium glutamate always helps me write a good paper. It starts vibrations going in my head."

My term paper was due the next morning, on Kafka: I had been trying for three months to invent a convincing thesis about the ethics of transformation, or, why it might be better to be a cockroach.

I stared at the back of Ben's head. If I didn't get the paper done I would fail the course and my grade point average would be too low to let me qualify for the junior-year-abroad program. Ben's haircut was noticeably ragged; in one place there was a bare spot big as a dime. I'd been cutting the back of his hair all semester—I never touched the front since he was very proud of one long curl which hung over his forehead. I had sworn never to tell anyone that he used styling mousse on it. I used nothing but Ivory soap on my own short curly hair; the mousse was left over from Naomi, his girlfriend, who was spending her junior year in Leningrad. Everyone at the university who had any pretensions to knowledge felt he or she had to spend his or her junior year abroad; it was as essential as being against apartheid. It was like a disease. Right in the middle of college life it hit you: a person had to drop everything, leave all friends, leap on a plane, and start walking around in narrow foreign streets, reading signs in peculiar languages. The rationale was that travel was broadening; the experience was guaranteed to give you perspective. It showed a person how crass and materialistic we were here in America, how self-centered, how narrow, but also—after seeing how awful it was elsewhere—how lucky we were to live here. I had been told in the first orientation meeting on Austria that I would come to this realization and it would make my entire future life in America a happier one.

I don't know why I had picked Austria—I had to pick some place and I loved Viennese waltzes. I had also studied German—a language which reminded me of my grandmother's voice when she used to speak to me in Yiddish. I thought of how, when I was little, she always said: "Sitz by mir," and this would make me tearful. Other reasons I chose Austria: Freud came from there and he was smart; they have good pastries.

Naomi and Ben had been in love and had slept together all their sophomore year. But then it came time for her to jump on the plane and go beyond the pale. Ben was too poor to participate in the junior-year-abroad program, but he said that travel was not considered all that important for engineers.

7

Although Naomi was now gone and Ben hardly mentioned her unless he got a letter (which he would read to me), I assumed she would inevitably come back, as most junior-year-abroad people did, unless she was sent to a gulag or decided to make a life with the Russian guide she'd met on a tour of the Kremlin. Ben was worried that Naomi might corrupt the man by transforming him into a radical capitalist—then, when she left, he would be ruined, dreaming forever of unattainable Levis and VCRs.

"I'd rather be transformed into a capitalist than a cockroach," I said.

"What?"

"Do you think my mother is trying to tell me something by sending me that mammogram?" My mother's breasts were exactly the size of the one in the picture.

Ben turned around. He looked at my face. He said, "I think your mother just does weird things to pass the time, like the rest of us. How many shrimp do you think we'll require for our tempura bash? How many do you think the average person eats?" He took his solar calculator out of the desk drawer and slid it under his lamp. "I guess it depends on how big they are," he advised himself.

I flopped down on my bed and covered my head with my down comforter. At times I thought Ben had invited me to move into his room for the down comforter alone. I didn't really know what he craved from me. What I craved from him, besides attention, was interpretation. Because he was a chemical engineer, I thought he might take a different slant on things and see in human acts meanings I hadn't even thought of. I couldn't begin to guess how a chemical engineer might see the world. I didn't even know what they did after graduation. Ben didn't seem to know exactly either. "I'll cross that bridge when I come to it," he said. "But it's a sure thing."

I knew that Ben and I had nothing in common, but most of the time it didn't seem important. Who cared that while we were in our mothers' wombs our brains had developed in absolutely opposite directions? It was quite enough for me to be wrapped warmly with him every night in my down comforter. No wisdom available to me seemed to apply—I just loved being with him. I had no idea what would happen when Naomi came home from Russia, or when I was forced to leave for Austria. But that seemed like worrying about what would happen after graduation. The A-bomb could fall first.

We went to the White Panda Palace that night, where I ordered mu-shu pork and urged Ben to order shrimp in lobster sauce. Whenever I could, I ate pork and shrimp, delicacies which had been denied me in my childhood, along with mushrooms, due to my mother's ethics about what should be eaten in a Jewish home. Our fortune cookies were already on the table beside two pairs of splintery chopsticks. I chose one and cracked it open.

"Listen to this, Ben. This is eerie. 'You will step on the soil of many countries.'" I watched his face for some response. I wanted him to beg me not to go to Austria, to tell me, as my mother did, that it was no place for a Jewish girl. To tell me that he would die without me. Ben was busy reading his own fortune. He crumpled it up and tossed it in the ashtray.

"I hate secretive people."

"Fortune cookies are nonsense, Annie," he said.

"You never know," I said. "I have all of mine taped up on my wall."

"Along with your bellybutton," he said. "I can't believe your mother really saved your bellybutton for you all these years and sent it to you on your birthday in a jewelry case!" **9**

"She thinks it's very special—like the caul lifted from the head of a blessed child."

"Your mother is spacey," he said. "Your wall is spacey."

"My wall is an art form," I said. "It's not so different from what's on display in the art gallery right now."

Ben spun the soy sauce bottle. Then he sprinkled a few grains of sugar on the tabletop and tried to balance the edge of the bottle on them. After a tense few seconds, he succeeded.

"Magic," I said, approvingly.

"Laws of physics," he said, with a tinge of annoyance.

"Ben," I said, "I'm really afraid to go to Austria and leave my mother."

"Leave her? You're not even with her!"

"But I don't want fate to separate us. Who knows if I'd ever see her again?"

The waiter brought Ben's hot-and-sour soup, and he began spooning it into his mouth with a pink plastic spoon shaped like a platypus's tail. I retrieved Ben's fortune from the ashtray and uncrumpled it without asking permission. It said: "You will reunite with an old love very soon."

A dog was getting electrocuted on a tightrope just inside the door of the art gallery. Three times that semester I had dragged Ben to the Jonathan Borofsky exhibit. This time I told him I needed to view it with the intention of tying Borofsky's approach into my Kafka paper. I told him Borofsky was a living master of significant transformation. When I walked in the door, I had the feeling I had come back to my own little planet where it was possible to breathe. Flares of flame shot from the dog's prancing paws. Back and forth he went on the video screen, dancing on the burning wire, his paws on fire.

"I feel just like that," I confessed to Ben, and immediately put my head against his shoulder. Whenever something moved me deeply, I liked to assume Ben was also touched and that our souls were in harmony. Because Ben had an agreeable smile, I could imagine we were in harmony nearly all the time if I wanted to. We were standing in front of the bearded clown in the red top hat. She wore a white ballerina's skirt, a blue bodice, and pink toe shoes. A machine inside kept one toe spinning. A person could stare into its face for a long time and not get restless.

From hidden speakers came the low rumble of the chattering men. These men, clones of one another, stood all around the gallery, their hinged jaws chattering. Ben checked his back pocket for his aspirin. He took out the plastic bottle, leaving a ghost of its shape in the threads of his jeans. He held up the bottle to count the pills.

"Getting low," he said nervously.

I took the bottle and put it in the ballerina's hand. "This would fit right in," I told Ben. "Leave it there. Your contribution to art."

Ben snatched the bottle away and went to find some water. He thought he was a drug-free person, but he didn't understand the scope of these things. Freed of his presence, I began to move around the gallery at my own pace. Little phrases from the exhibits began to pile up in my mind:

"You are alone."

"Slow down."

"There is no one to please but your—"

"She was found smothered in her crib, she was truly loved by her Dad . . ."

"Mom, I lost the election."

"I realized that if I was going to make it I would need some help . . ."

"Littering is an indication of a sick mind."

"Feel free to play."

A couple was playing ping-pong on one of the exhibits, a gaudy green thing with USA painted on it. The man kept talking to the woman—he could have been a work of art, his jaw flapping like a chattering man. I stood in front of a portrait of Elvis Presley, which was cut in half. Under my feet were flyers, littering the gallery, part of the display. I took my fortune cookie prediction out of my pocket and threw it on the floor, kicking it around to mingle with the art work. Then I started to look around for Ben. Sometimes a sense of panic grasped me when he was away too long; I would fear that he had run back to the co-op, barred the door, and taken my down comforter hostage. Then I would have to go back to Sylvia Cohen's room and beg her to evict her boyfriend so that I could move back in. I went downstairs to where the restrooms were, and there I found Ben next to the water fountain, sitting on a concrete bench shaped like a tree stump.

"Are you okay?"

"I'm enjoying Borofsky's art work," he said. He patted the tree stump. He smiled. "I think my headache's going away."

"That's not part of the display," I said. "It's just a low-maintenance chair. It's been here forever."

"I thought it was art."

"That's how much you know," I said, astonished at the fury in my voice.

"Can we go home now?" Ben asked.

"Not yet," I said meanly. "I have a little more research to

do." I left his side and went upstairs. I found myself between the legs of Borofsky's huge bubble man, a floor-to-ceiling creature bent like a praying mantis, motors working his huge cellophane thighs. From the awe I felt within me, I thought I had finally come face-to-face with some religious essence. On the nearby wall the artist had written: "I dreamed that some Hitler-type person was not allowing everyone to roller skate in public places . . . but was informed that Hitler had been dead a long time." I got down beside the bubble man and tried to imitate his submissive posture. I realized that if I went to Austria for my junior abroad, I would surely not be allowed to roller skate.

12

I stood up and was suddenly face-to-face with a framed painting of a daisy. "Don't," it said.

How simple. How easy for an artist to make pronouncements which pretended to penetrate mystery. Borofsky could put a pile of numbers in a display case and call it art. He could scribble cryptic, puzzling, poetic words on the wall. He could pretend to have deciphered the essence of childhood by saying, "Mom, I lost the election. Buddy Rifkin won . . . ," and have a little boy diving headfirst down the spiral body of a snake. If he had dreamed his mother's head was being drilled open by a bandit, he could have framed the page from his dream book and hung it up in the gallery. Who but an artist could create a dog dancing over tongues of fire on a high wire and then go home— leaving the animal there turning to cinders in the video glow when the gallery closed for the night?

But I had to live in the world, grow up, die. I had to move out of Ben's room, say goodbye to him, and see what happened next—in Austria or wherever. I had to write my impressions of Gregor Samsa's pain in order to get a grade in order to get a degree in order to get a job in order to be the kind of woman no man would be obliged to have to take care of.

I'd rather have been an artist. Then all I'd have had to do would be to hang my bellybutton, my fortune cookie, and the blue-and-white mammogram on the wall with my mother's words over them like a benediction:

"Man's Fate."

13

SEE BONNIE & CLYDE
DEATH CAR

. . . .

At midnight, when the temperature in the Sahara Tower registers 102 degrees, two ducks make a landing on the Astroturf around the pool and slip silently into the water. The moon, lying on the pool's surface like a tiny frozen marble, remains undisturbed.

Lynn, who is reclining on a white plastic lounge chair, finds all of this astonishing: the searing heat at midnight, the magical appearance of the ducks (where did they come from? why don't they react to the powerful chlorine fumes rising from the water?), the immutability of the moon's image, her lack of hunger. Do the laws of physics and biology not apply in Las Vegas?

Phil has been at the same blackjack table from the moment they stumbled into the casino from the oven of the parking lot at four P.M.; neither of them has eaten anything since they shared a container of blueberry yogurt after noon, just beyond Barstow, while traveling at seventy-five miles an hour past deformed Joshua trees and empty lake beds. When the plastic spoon broke, Lynn had scooped the purple cream into Phil's mouth with her finger.

She had been to Las Vegas once, five years before, with another man, and had vowed never to come again because it seemed to her the place to end things. At least she had come to the end of her money then, and to the end of her friendship with the man.

Now she is here by default; Phil's suitcase had been packed for another kind of trip, to visit his father in San Francisco, where three days before he had been paralyzed

by a stroke. Lynn had desperately not wanted to go with
Phil, to attend at yet another hospital bedside. For the last
month—till the funeral last Wednesday—she had spent
nearly every evening beside the bed of a friend dying of
AIDS, a man who had worked at her newspaper and with
whom she often had lunch. Since then (she knew it wasn't
rational) her fear of illness had assumed phobic propor-
tions. Just when she most needed a rest from facing the
void, Phil wanted her along. *"I want you with me through
thick and thin,"* he said. *"In sickness and health,"* he
added. The words seemed significant to her, so, hopefully,
16 she packed her suitcase. Except that just as they were
walking out the door there was a phone call from Phil's
mother. They each picked up an extension.

"Don't come now, wait until Dad is stabilized, the doctor
thinks a week or so later would be better. We'll know more
then, anyway."

When Phil put down the phone, his face was soft and
miserable. "God—I'm all packed. What am I supposed to
do *now?*" he was holding his car keys in his hand.

"We could always just go on a vacation for the weekend,"
she said. "As long as we get back in time for work on
Monday."

He stared at her peculiarly; his expression was unreada-
ble and her heart skipped a beat.

"Phil, listen—that's only a joke, a joke," she apologized.

"No," he said. "You're right. Why not? Why don't we go
to Vegas?"

"Why not, I suppose," she said. She sank down into the
beanbag chair she'd claimed on her last trip to see her
parents. The beads slid suddenly under her like quicksand.
How fast life's direction could change. "Do you think we
can get a hotel room?"

A roulette wheel was bolted to the reception desk at the
Sahara. The clerk told Lynn to give it a spin to see if she
could win a free or half-price room.

"Oh, too bad. Give it another whirl and see if you can do better," the woman urged after Lynn's spin had landed the pointer on the regular room rate. But even with a second chance Lynn got only $2.50 off.

Phil was looking with longing toward the noisy, red-lit casino, leaning his arms on the reception desk. The angle at which his head was reflected in the mirrored wall showed her how thin his hair was getting, how his sideburns (he still wore them) were of slightly different lengths. Well, why did she persist in noting these things? She knew his flaws, his habits, his limits; they were certainly not new to her. She wanted to marry this man; she would rush with him across the street to the Chapel of Happy Memories right now if she could get him to agree. Did it ever occur to him how she cared for him? To the point of requesting a hotel room no higher than the third or fourth floor? Further than that (she had read) the ladders of firemen did not reach.

She saw herself in the mirror—not a glamorous woman, no longer so young. Phil was an unambitious man; worried, nervous, steady, old beyond his years. But she wanted him. It was this knowledge which shaped her mind these days.

After spending hours in the casino, she has come out here to the pool to find quiet. The pair of ducks glide in parallel lines for short distances, then turn and return to where they started from. One of them lets a pellet drop from his body; it snakes through the green water, falling slowly. The two birds glide and turn, glide and turn. They could be swans, they are so graceful. Lynn thinks ahead to mid-morning tomorrow, when the heat will distort the air and the Sahara Tower will show a temperature of 110; who will ever guess that wild creatures swam here last night?

Lynn and a woman have a tug-of-war over a stool between two rows of slot machines, but she relents and lets her have it because she's older than Lynn and looks poor. However, the woman is playing a twenty-five-cent slot while Lynn is

17

taking her chances with only nickels. She definitely is afraid to play quarters; she's already bought one roll of quarters, ten dollars for forty—and, at five coins a pull (she believes in playing for the highest wins as long as she's playing), she gets only eight pulls and the money's gone. No, she can't throw away ten dollars that fast. Silver dollars would be worse. They'd shoot away and turn to quicksilver in the molten heat of the machines.

For a while she stands at Phil's shoulder as he makes bets with two five-dollar chips at a time, sometimes four, but that's his privilege; he's in another sphere, his father is newly paralyzed. He's entitled to play for high stakes. When he loses two hands in a row, she fears she's changing his luck and wanders away, up and down the aisles of lit and beckoning machines.

She tries a video slot: "I'm loose as a goose," the screen tells her as she puts three nickels in and pulls the arm. Nothing lines up. The machine announces, in red letters, "Game's over. But you look like a winner. Columbus took a chance. Try again." This time three bells show up on the center line and, for a moment, the bells turn into the smiling mustachioed faces of little men—then ten nickels come tumbling down into the tin bowl. Lynn is pleased even though by now a muscle in her right shoulder is burning and her fingers are black from handling the coins. She's getting good at breaking open packets of nickels; expertly she knocks the roll on the lip of the bowl. When it splits, she pushes out the coins from either end with her two index fingers. She's fast. She can put five nickels into a machine without missing a beat; she can put them in *two* machines and pull the handles at once, doubling her chances at the big hit. She enjoys certain diversions she practices (she thinks they are her own invention). For instance, if she drops a coin on the floor, she will wait till the reels are spinning and then kneel to retrieve it. It's her hope that she'll hit a jackpot (without even watching for one) and the machine will spit out a stream of money; she wants to be down there, on her knees, to see her fortune come out of the spout. She wants to be eye-to-eye with her luck as it pours out at her like a silver waterfall.

It's so late that she's lightheaded, feeling weird. There are no clocks in the casino. In the cocktail lounge a Madonna look-alike stands in front of an electronic keyboard singing "I'm gonna keep my baby." Her cleavage shimmers, but it looks innocent on her thin body. The floor vibrates from deep inside. Despite the music, the shouts from the craps tables, the clack of the wheel-of-fortune, the shrieks of the jackpot winners, Lynn feels as she once did at a church service, when a Bach organ prelude shook the wooden pew sending a sexual thrill through her. She ought to have a headache—but she does not. Shouldn't Phil quit and come to bed? In their apartment he gets tired before eleven. Oughtn't they to eat? Have the ducks flown away yet? Were the two of them going south for the winter but instead decided to stay here, in this aberrant, overheated city? She would go outside again to see, but she doesn't want to lose her chance to be lucky. If she misses her lucky pull, she'll never be a winner. So she stays and plays; she's allowed herself a week's salary in nickels, if need be. To win big one has to take big risks. The thin singer flashes her rhinestones, clutches her mike, and belts out, "I wanna know what love is . . ."

Finally Phil comes to find Lynn. He must have hit a losing streak, but she doesn't ask. They take the elevator up, leaning against the sides, eyes nearly closed. In their room they fall into bed. They don't even touch fingers they're so tired.

Even with the extra-heavy drapes on the window, knives of morning sunlight manage to slice through and pierce their sleep. They wake shielding their eyes. The thumping from below can be felt already; it seems to come up through

19

the pipes, an urgent force from the red-carpeted, neon-lighted, all-night room. The casino calls to Lynn's mind an emergency room in a hospital, always open and ready. Casualties of love and war eagerly accepted.

While Phil showers, she hefts her little paper cup of nickels and estimates she has about four dollars' worth left. She's impatient; men take so long to shave. She glances through a throwaway she found on an ashtray in the hallway last night: *Las Vegas Bachelor Guide:* "Triple X-Rated Nude Dancers Direct To Your Room." "Free Limo Service To All Brothels." "The World-Famous Historic Chicken Ranch—The Best Little Whorehouse In The West."

20

She settles down in a chair to read:

> *What do a nutritionist and a classical pianist have in common? For one thing both women work at the Chicken Ranch and, like all the other ladies of the ranch, are accomplished, intelligent women with a wide variety of interests. The women, who range from 18 to 37, have skills in such areas as nursing, teaching, real estate, farming, and finance. One of the ladies speaks five languages and is still studying. Though far away from their homes, they support the local Pahrump senior citizens' center, which indicates their caring support of their home away from home.*

Lynn thinks of how boring her job at the paper has become, how poorly it pays. What if she went out to the Chicken Ranch for an interview? There is a free flight, the paper says, from Vegas to Pahrump.

> *The Chicken Ranch features a new eight-person jacuzzi offering private and group relaxation and enjoyment.*

She considers suggesting that perhaps Phil should take that free plane. Does she want him to have *that* much fun? She's been tired and unimaginative in bed for some time now, for at least as long as it took her friend to die. But she wants everyone to get as happy as possible. She wants to be genial toward the world these days, forgiving, generous. Everyone is struggling—who is she to judge anyone? Tears actually fill her eyes when she reads:

> *The new wing at the Chicken Ranch is fully equipped to handle physically handicapped people with everything from the wheelchair ramp on the front porch to the specially designed lavatory facilities. Doors have been widened throughout for the comfort and pleasure of all visitors.*

The pictures in the pamphlet show girls in silk teddies, g-strings, and lace garter belts. All Lynn has in her suitcase is her Mickey Mouse sleepshirt since she thought she'd be sleeping at Phil's parents' house, possibly—if circumstances demanded it—alone in the guest room.

Phil comes out of the bathroom in a cloud of steam. With his hair wet, he's closer to bald than she's ever seen him. She goes to him and hugs him tightly, her few tears mixing with the drops of water still on his chest.

"I'm ready to go down," he says with a smile, letting go of her. "Maybe we'll have energy for a little hug later on."

"I hope so," she says.

He indicates a pile of red chips on the top of the TV. "I think I'm actually a little ahead," he announces.

"That's wonderful," she says. "I'm happy for you."

In a room as big as a gymnasium, the breakfast buffet (with the fifty-cents-off coupon from their fun books) costs only $2.50; for this they get herring in sour cream, bagels and lox, omelets, blueberry muffins, Danish, doughnuts, coffee. On the warming tray are chicken livers in gravy, chipped creamed beef, and blueberry blintzes. On another table is an array of fruits: grapefruit, watermelon, prunes, peaches, grapes, plums.

Lynn and Phil stuff themselves—they are both severely starved—while inspecting the hotel guests at the other tables. Everyone seems to be eating from at least two full plates. Everyone seems to weigh at least two hundred pounds. The women are dressed mainly in bright polyester floral pantsuits; the men tend to wear cowboy shirts and string ties. Each person has some piece of gold jewelry adorning his body somewhere.

Lynn wears no rings at all. Her only decoration is her digital watch with Clark Gable on its face. She doesn't glance at it; whatever day, whatever date it is, she doesn't want to know. She's caught up in the spirit of nowhereness, she deeply appreciates it.

"Should I call my mother?" Phil says.

"No," Lynn answers truthfully. "What for? Not now."

They decide to make a run for Lots o'Slots, which is right across the streeet. "Hang on," Phil says, and pulls her through the double glass doors into the oven of morning. She breathes through her mouth, hoping to cool the air before it sears her lungs. At the bus stop, a man is asleep on a bench, clutching a paper bag in his hand. Beside the bench is his wheelchair. Lynn sees he is lacking legs. But at that moment Phil yells, "Look!" and from above them a human form hurtles down a vertical chute from six or seven floors high into a pool of water.

"Would you go on that water slide?" Lynn asks.

"Only if you'd go with me," Phil says. "Would you?"

"I'd go with you anywhere," she says. "I'd stick with you through thick and thin." She can imagine them paying the admission to Wet 'n Wild, climbing the circular ramp high up into the heart of the sun, and then taking their places at the top of the chute, hands entwined.

She wants to do it, shake him into action. But he's squinting, shading his eyes as he watches a second person shoot down the chute. He isn't capable of grand acts. She needs to remember that.

Lots o'Slots has a front open to the street; hot air occupies the first ten feet of the casino area.

"See you," Phil says, and disappears toward the blackjack tables.

Lynn takes out her cup of nickels and finds a circle of machines under a sign which reads "Progressive Jackpot." The jackpot increases one penny by each pull of the slot arm on any one of the machines. The present kitty holds $4,320.59. Lynn deposits three coins (the maximum for the highest win) in a machine, and it spits back thirty nickels on the first pull. Good, she pulls up a stool, though the heat is at her back. This machine is near the entrance, maybe it's really set to give back 97 percent, maybe it's "generous."

23

Beside her a young woman is seated, leaning her head against the glass screen of her machine. Her hair is tangled ash-blonde. She's wearing blue jeans and a pink-and-blue T-shirt. Her eyes are closed; without looking she regularly inserts three nickels in the slot and pulls the handle. She takes the nickels from the tin bowl at the level of her knees, drops them in, pulls; takes out more nickels, drops, pulls. She functions like a sleepwalker. There are four reels spinning on these machines: no cherries, no bells, no oranges, no dollar signs, no little smiling men—just black bars and white spaces, like jail uniforms.

Lynn hits again! Three out of four mixed bars show in a row and thirty more coins come down. Lynn's heart leaps up. The machine even plays a little tune, as at the start of a horse race, when this happens: "Dah-dah, dadadada, dah-dah!" Thirty coins are good for ten free pulls, ten more chances, using the casino's money, for the big jackpot.

The woman beside Lynn gets a double-long fanfare. Sixty coins tumble down. "Hey, not bad," Lynn says. She'd like to make a friend here. But the woman is busy pulling again, her eyes still closed. This time two sevens line up and two bars.

"That's *really* close!" Lynn says.

The woman half-opens her eyes. "Yeah, really," she answers, but she doesn't even glance at Lynn. She just keeps putting in nickels. Lynn wonders: if two sevens out of four line up, does that mean one is halfway to paradise?

The woman is searching in her handbag now, searching quite desperately. She dumps its contents in her lap—wallet, glasses, cigarettes, tissues—till she finds one last roll of nickels. She kisses the grimy blue-and-white wrapper. Then she takes off her wedding ring and hangs it on the call-button, which is there to call the change-girl for more coins. She smashes open the roll of nickels and starts pumping them in. She's crying. Her back is shaking and she's sobbing. For some reason, Lynn begins to cry, too. They both work hard for a long time with no music from the machine to encourage them. They go faster and faster. The laws of probability seem quite cruel, quite indifferent to their needs.

Thunk, thunk, space, space. Only two bars, not three, line up. *Space, thunk, thunk, thunk.* Three bars, but at the wrong end of the line. Playing here is like living. Nothing works out most of the time.

Lynn is almost out of coins. She has three three-nickel pulls left. Her buddy, who seems just about out, too, puts in one, two nickels, but hasn't a third. She scrapes the bottom of her handbag again, but there's nothing in there.

"It's all over," she states, looking upward, not to heaven, but to the jackpot sign, whose number has gone up by almost a dollar. Suddenly, like a snake, she slides off her stool and disappears out the door.

"Wait!" Lynn cries after her. Her wedding ring is still there, hanging on the button, a thin, plain little circle of gold. Lynn stands up to see if she can see her, to see if she's coming back. Maybe she went to get more money from someone, from her husband. But probably there is no husband. Lynn decides to put a paper cup over the slot handle to indicate the machine is taken; she will guard and protect it till the woman comes back.

But an hour later (Lynn has bought another twenty dollars' worth of nickels) the woman has not returned. A half-hour later Phil arrives at Lynn's back, ready to move on to some other casino.

"Look at this," Lynn says. She lifts the wedding ring from the button and holds it in front of Phil's face. "Someone went away and left this here."

He looks as if he doesn't recognize what it is.

25

"A wedding ring," she explains.

"Well, just leave it," he says.

"No, I want it," she says. "The woman isn't coming back."

"Then take it," Phil says. Behind them, a woman shrieks and jumps into the air. "Hey! A thousand dollars," Phil remarks. "That lady just won a thousand dollars, Lynn."

"Give me just one lucky nickel," Lynn asks. She puts the woman's wedding ring on her own ring finger. She is going to play the woman's last pull and will accept the result as an omen. If she wins the big jackpot with it, her life will change and she will be happy forever.

Phil hands her a nickel. She puts it in and pulls for dear life. But she doesn't watch. She walks out to the street with Phil and listens raptly for the tune, for the rhapsody, for the celestial music she dreams of. But all she hears is the tinny thunk-thunk of the thin winnings of other human beings.

The sun is setting over the desert when they leave Las Vegas for LA; they're blinded by the light. The clouds turn into sparklers, the sky ahead is an inferno, they can't go on. Just on their right, at the state line, is one last casino called Whiskey Pete's. The marquee announces:

SEE BONNIE & CLYDE DEATH CAR
95 CENT BREAKFAST
10 oz. CHOICE NY STEAK $2.50

"Let's stop in the casino there," Phil says. "We can wait for the sun to set."

"Good," Lynn answers. "Maybe I'll be lucky."

Instead, within five minutes, she loses her purse. She puts it down between two slot machines and then wanders away with her cup of coins to some other machine. When she realizes it's gone, she gasps like a person who has won a jackpot. All the rows of blinking slots look alike: she's lost.

She dashes like a crazy woman up and down the aisles, confiding breathlessly to every passing cowboy and change-girl, "I lost my purse." She runs, she runs and looks in the dark crevices between machines where she finds ashtrays, empty cocktail glasses, blackened paper cups, handy-wipe wrappers, and the curls of torn-open paper coin rolls.

"Oh God!" She can't believe she's done something this stupid. Her purse, that puffy brown kangaroo-pouch full of her precious cards and keys and her silver whistle and her money and her can of mace: gone. *Where are you?* she thinks. *Why don't you call my name?* She sees Phil bent over his blackjack hand at a table with four other men who are bent over their hands. Luck, luck, everyone wants luck and she's sick of luck!

Is *she* lucky? She didn't die of AIDS, did she? She escaped seeing Phil's paralyzed father, she even has a wedding ring now she never had before. Is that luck?

Suddenly she nearly falls on her face over a platform displaying an ancient automobile she didn't notice on the way in. The car is roped off and is riddled with bullet holes. A life-sized picture of Bonnie Parker in a long black dress is mounted on thick cardboard and is leaning against the front of the car. A companion photo shows Clyde Barrow, handsome and shrewd, holding a machine gun and

sitting on the front bumper of what must be a Ford. For also
on display is a letter addressed to Mr. Henry Ford, Detroit,
Michigan, received there on April 13, 1934:

> *Dear Sir:—*
> *While I still have got breath in my lungs I
> will tell you what a dandy car you make. I have
> drove Fords exclusivly when I could get away
> with one. For sustained speed and freedom from
> trouble the Ford has got ever other car skinned
> and even if my business hasen't been strickly
> legal it don't hurt eny-thing to tell you what a
> fine car you got in the V8—*
>
> *Yours truly*
> *Clyde Champion Barrow*

27

She studies the car in which the lovers were shot to death
in an ambush in Gibsland, Louisiana, on May 23, 1934.
Now that's love she thinks. *That's sticking together through
thick and thin.*

Someone taps her on the back. She turns and finds Phil
behind her, looking as handsome as Clyde Barrow and
holding in his hand, awkwardly, as men hold purses, hers.

"Oh my God! Where did you find it?" She kisses him,
jumping up and down, as he tells, happily, some garbled
story about a woman who found it, brought it to the blackjack table where her husband was playing, how Phil
claimed it as Lynn's . . .

It's only a purse. But she adores it and she adores Phil
and she knows she has luck because she's just been rescued
from a dark wood.

"Holy shit," Phil says, his arm around her, patting her
shoulder. "Look at those bullet holes. Look at that smashed
windshield. Will you look at that?"

"They really must have loved each other," Lynn says.
Her purse, soft and padded, feels like a baby in her arms.

"That's what I call living hard and fast," Phil says en-
viously.

"That's what I call having fun till the very end," Lynn says.

"Like us," Phil says, giving her a hug. "You think maybe like us?"

28

CHICKEN SKIN
SANDWICHES

In 1950 my father met a man named Jim Bucks who had a little money and wanted to finance my father's inventions. My father thought he knew of a way to get maple syrup to run out of trees faster than anyone had ever done before, and Jim Bucks was working on getting access to a forest of maple trees on which they could experiment. Although my mother was usually suspicious of the men my father befriended, she went out of her way to impress Jim Bucks by playing the Minute Waltz for him on our Knabe grand piano. When she finished performing for him one night after dinner as my father and Aunt Hilda and my grandmother sat listening, Jim Bucks, in his striped shirt with gold cufflinks, applauded so loudly with the pink, thick palms of his hands that I had to cover my ears.

This was a time of relative peace in our household; the war had finally ended and its repercussions, at least as far as we were concerned, were fading away. My mother had conceived and borne another child, my fat-cheeked sister Carol, whose arrival soothed her grief, in part, over the baby she had lost during the war when she and my father had been in Florida. She had miscarried on a troop train coming back to Brooklyn after my father was notified that he had to get a defense job at home or be drafted.

Although the trip to Miami Beach had been intended as a winter vacation, a period of privacy long promised to my mother, it was there that my father first put into action his talent for inventiveness. He had been struck with the idea of a business tailored to the needs of the war while sitting in the lobby of our hotel, the Mellow Vista, which was mainly occupied by soldiers. Daily he observed the soldiers struggling to write letters on hotel stationery, which was pale pink and had two brown palm trees on it. I often sat at the long table in the lobby with the soldiers, drawing on a piece of stationery while they sat with their heads in their hands, thinking of what to write in their letters home.

My father believed he could solve their problems. He did some scouting around in Miami and brought back a machine which cut phonograph records, its thick needle designed to carve spiral springs of black plastic thread as it turned round and round on coated paper discs. He rented a tiny store on Collins Avenue and had a sign painted which read: *SEND YOUR VOICE HOME TO YOUR MOM! TO YOUR BEST GIRL!* He furnished the store with a desk and chair; he set up a small, cozy booth with a brown curtain for privacy in which a soldier could sit or stand as he spoke his thoughts into the microphone before he was shipped out to fight in the war.

My father let me sit on a stool in the store, collecting plastic thread as it spun off the records. It sprung about in my hands as if it had a life of its own. My mother, who had always been skeptical of my father's inventions, developed a new respect for him as the little business began reaping profits. She, with her musical bent, suggested that my father buy a ukulele in order that soldiers who found it too hard to think of something to say might instead strum a little tune or sing a song on the record. My mother and father had begun to whisper together about staying in Florida and not going home at all, but buying a second recording machine and a piano which my mother could play while the soldiers sang to their sweethearts in the privacy of the curtained booth.

My mother gave herself freely to her music—she played the piano with surprising gentleness and emotion. I was grateful for a chance to see her in this soft submission because in our real life together she was nervous and defensive and distant. In Brooklyn my father had loved to sing while she played his favorite songs: "I'll Take You Home Again, Kathleen," and "Danny Boy." To me he liked to sing "You Are My Sunshine." For herself she preferred Beethoven, Schubert, and Chopin.

My mother was passionate about privacy, never having had any during her marriage except for the vacation trip to Florida in the midst of the war. At home in Brooklyn we lived with my unmarried Aunt Hilda and my grandmother. We all shared a little house with a lilac tree in the front yard and a peach tree in the back. I found the arrangement quite agreeable; my grandmother had infinite patience with me and was anxious to teach me the complicated procedures involved in cooking *kreplach* and *tzimmes*, while Aunt Hilda, who earned money by running a beauty parlor in our closed-in sunporch, always made me welcome when she did a manicure or a permanent. I loved the variety of life in that house; if my mother was irritable or having a migraine, I would join my grandmother for a cooking lesson, or plunk myself down in the beauty parlor and watch Aunt Hilda's competent fingers push at the cuticles of one of her lady customers with a smooth wooden stick, making a little pale moon appear at the base of each nail. Sometimes while she was giving a permanent she allowed me to dip the chemical paper rolls, which looked like small cigars, into a bowl of hot water, then took them from me quickly as they began to sizzle lest I get burned. When she did haircuts, I marveled at the way she could select her comb or scissors or thinning shears from the pocket of her apron without looking down. She bent backwards like a dancer while she gave haircuts, sighting in some magical way at her customer's hairline, intent on making every hair even with the one beside it.

My mother thought it was not healthy for me to be breathing in the smell of nail polish every day. She hated

31

the sight of the women's dark hairs which lay twisted and
wet in the upstairs bathroom sink after Aunt Hilda gave
shampoos; my mother also feared that the gossip I listened
to in the beauty shop—amazing tales of childbirth and evil-
hearted men—would warp my mind. She wanted my father's inventions to make us rich so we could move away,
buy a new house of our own, and have privacy.

My father didn't seem to mind our living arrangements as
much as she did; he kidded a lot with my grandmother and
complimented her on her snow-white hair and her delicious
honey cake. He gave her a pair of heart-shaped diamond
earrings from his antique shop and said she looked in them
like the Queen of England. He teased Aunt Hilda about her
tiny waist, her graceful collar bones, her delicate hands,
and ignored the fact that her skin was very bad. When my
mother began to enter one of her moods, which could
escalate from a complaint about my not eating to a tantrum
during which she threatened to lock herself in the
bathroom and take iodine, my father would dip his head at
me to indicate *Go, Scram, Vamoose* and I would knock
back my chair and run to Aunt Hilda's side and let her take
me upstairs and keep me out of danger till my mother got
tired of yelling and lay down in her bed with a cold cloth on
her head.

Jim Bucks wanted to take my father away to New
Hampshire for ten days. He had arranged to borrow the
maple woods of a friend, and he wanted my father to apply
his ingenuity and concentration to the syrup project without interruption. My mother, who hated to let him go far,
was agreeable this time. She was busy with the new baby
and seemed to think that Jim Bucks was legitimate. He was
a short, dapper man with a neat blond mustache and
alligator shoes. He had wandered into my father's antique
shop and offered my father a twenty-dollar bill for the
contents of the teacup of loose change my father kept on the

32

counter. My father warned him he'd lose money, but Jim
Bucks had just laughed and insisted he wanted to take a
chance. After the deal was made, Jim Bucks counted out
the quarters and half-dollars and nickels and dimes, and
found that he had made himself a five-dollar profit.

After that he and my father were good friends. He came
to eat at our house, bringing me boxes of spearmint
Chiclets, and he flirted with Aunt Hilda, just enough to
please her, but not enough to threaten her. We all knew she
wouldn't be interested in him anyway because he wasn't
Jewish. She often told me she was content not to be married; that living in the house with me and my sister made
her feel as if she had children of her own, and living in the
house with my sweet father made her feel as if she had a
husband of her own.

33

My mother was very charming to Jim Bucks; she laughed
a lot in his presence, perhaps believing that he was her
ticket to a house of her own. The antique store made a bare
living, but only that, nothing more. The trip to Florida
during the war had been her only time alone with my father
and me, without having my grandmother and aunt hovering
in the background.

In the summer of 1950, even though we were still as
crowded in the house as ever, even though my grandmother
infuriated my mother by opening her bedroom door every
morning to collect laundry from under the bed, my mother
had other things to think about besides privacy—the new
baby and polio.

Polio was a wide green bug with dancing red eyes. It
lurked in the water fountain at the playground and on the
handlebars of other children's bicycles. It was on the wing-
tips of the seagulls at the beach, on the armrests of the
dentist's chair, and in the Good Humor Man's ice-cream
bars. I was not allowed to go anywhere other than our
front yard and backyard during the summer of 1950. My
Girl Scout troop was taking a boat trip to Bear Mountain;

my best friend Harriet went, but I was not allowed to go. I hung around the house, annoyed at my sister, who woke from her naps in a fierce temper and cried for an hour or two afterward. I was bored. I was tired of making *kreplach*, and I wished something exciting would happen. My mother intimated that soon something very exciting would happen. She had let my father go to New Hampshire to contemplate speeding the maple syrup out of the trees. She seemed almost lighthearted.

Harriet brought me back a pine cone from Bear Mountain, but my mother would not let me touch it, fearing it had some foreign germs on it. She made Harriet leave it on the railing of the wooden gate to the yard. Harriet, who had the happiest, most infectious laugh I had ever heard, was my only friend who could beat me at playing jacks; she had beautiful red hair and freckles; she talked to me through the screen door (as my mother held the handle to keep it firmly closed) and told me that our troop hadn't had a very good time on the trip and that I shouldn't feel too bad about having missed it. Mrs. Gargano, our leader, had cut herself on her Girl Scout knife, showing the troop how to carve chopsticks out of twigs. And Eleanor Weiss had caught poison oak. When Harriet left, my mother hugged me and told me that I was lucky not to have gone.

She talked about luck all the time. Women who lived with their families in houses of their own were lucky. Harriet's mother, who lived in a house across the street with her husband and Harriet, was an example of a lucky woman. My mother (my mother felt) was an example of an unlucky woman. If only she could be free of my aunt and my grandmother! If only my grandfather had not died; if only Aunt Hilda had married.

My sister was always screaming, her red mouth open and her tongue flailing. It was a long summer. My father came back, not having solved the mystery of slow-flowing maple syrup. But he had invented something else during the long hours in the car with Jim Bucks. His new idea would be a ride called the Merry-Go-Bob, which he hoped they could build at Coney Island next to the Parachute Jump. People who rode it would stand on little wedge-shaped pies on a circular floor which revolved like a merry-go-round. Above them would hang an immense arrow. It would be like a human wheel-of-fortune. The ride would end suddenly. Whichever wedge the arrow clicked to rest above would be the winning wedge. The lucky riders on that section of the pie would win prizes.

Jim Bucks and my father often sat at the dining room table till late at night, drawing pictures and making plans. **35** My grandmother, coming around the table with her silver crumb catcher tray and her little sable brush, would cluck at them and tell them that getting rich was not everything in life. Aunt Hilda, sitting on the couch, knitting a sweater, would smile in the warm cone of light from the standing brass lamp. My mother would pace back and forth in the kitchen, her heels clicking on the linoleum, her face alert. Upstairs, alone in the bedroom I shared with her, the baby would yell, demanding attention. I loved having Jim Bucks visit our house; my mother never once in that period threatened to take iodine.

One night Jim Bucks and my father invented chicken skin sandwiches. When my grandmother rendered chicken fat in a heavy pan over a low heat, with a bit of onion in it, the pieces of chicken skin would brown and turn crispy like bacon (which we were not allowed by my grandmother to have in the house). The fried skins, which my grandmother called *grevens*, were so delicious that Jim Bucks and my father decided they would open a food stand in Coney Island next to the Merry-Go-Bob. They laughed as they discussed what to call their chicken skin sandwiches; Jim Bucks thought Fakin'-Bacon would be a good name. They imagined themselves becoming as famous as Nathan's Hot

Dogs. For several nights they rendered the fat from chicken skins in our kitchen till the yellow smell of chicken fat hung over my hair like a pall. They made sample sandwiches and went around the neighborhood offering them to our neighbors who were sitting out on their stoops to get a breath of cool evening air. Jim Bucks and my father were like jolly madmen. An evening hardly went by without their inventing a new item.

Soon they were down in the basement, building a hockey game in a wooden box with carved players whose movements could be controlled by wooden knobs on the outside **36** of the box. By spinning the knobs, my father and Jim Bucks would make the players holding hockey sticks swing and hit a wooden puck. Jim Bucks said he was definitely going to put this one into production. My grandmother wanted to know where he got his money—was he a bank robber? My father said he had never asked. The two men were together every night, murmuring and talking long after I had gone to bed. My mother suffered her lonely state very well; she was comforted by dreams of the future. She held the new baby on her shoulder and pulled me to her side, promising us a private playground in the backyard of the new house we would soon be buying.

My father's next inspiration was a device he named Stand-A-Plate; it was a flat rectangle of plastic with ridges in it designed to hold dinner plates in a standing position in a kitchen cabinet. He thought it was his greatest geniusstroke of all. Jim Bucks was wild about the idea; during dinner he clapped my father on the back and told him they were going to be on Easy Street from now on. He began making plans to get it patented and arrange for a factory to make a mold and produce it. My father went to see the president of Woolworth's, and by some miracle the man agreed to stock it in all their stores. The project was expedited with lightning speed. My mother began secretly reading the real estate ads in the newspaper. One day, breaking the rule of not letting me go far from the house because of the danger of polio, she took me with her to three Woolworth's stores, proudly pointing out to me and the salesgirls that the gleaming rows of brightly colored plastic Stand-A-Plates were my father's invention.

It didn't take long before we learned that returns had started coming in. Customers were complaining to Woolworth's that the Stand-A-Plates tipped over, breaking their precious dishes. My grandmother, who had been given a dozen of them in yellow plastic by my father, said she could have told him that herself, but she didn't want to hurt his feelings.

37

My mother got migraines nearly every day after this happened. Aunt Hilda seemed serene. She kept me close to her when she could and taught me all she knew about cutting hair. She gave me a little tortoise-shell box containing a nail file with a mother-of-pearl handle, a nail buffer made of ivory and suede, and some emery boards. She enclosed a card that said: *Be good sweet maid and let who will be clever. Stay as sweet and dainty as you are. You are the darling of my life.*

The Stand-A-Plates were tipping over all over America, and they came back to my father from Woolworth's in daily shipments. Railway Express trucks stopped at our house every morning. Crates of Stand-A-Plates were piling up to the ceiling in our basement. Then—more trouble: my father learned from the toy stores which were selling the hockey game that the wooden knobs came off the box or got stuck and wouldn't turn; they were sorry, but they would stick to stocking Monopoly.

My father, who still took the subway every day to downtown Brooklyn to his antique store, began to work on one last idea. Jim Bucks had stopped coming to dinner, so my father talked to the rest of us about it. His face looked a little weary, but his blue-green eyes were lively. My mother played with her food and was not so attentive to him as she used to be. He was sure this new one was a winner. He was thinking about all the time people wasted waiting for the train. He was going to write to Sears Roebuck suggesting they install their mail-order catalogs in every subway station in America—on long tables, with chained-on pencils and piles of order forms. People waiting for the trains would browse and order millions of dollars' worth of goods.

A few nights later, the same night my father finished drafting his letter to Sears, my mother presented to us *her* invention. We were sitting in the living room after dinner; my grandmother was sewing up a hem on one of my mother's dresses, and Aunt Hilda was pressing flowers in her scrapbook, letting me help her. My father, smoking his pipe which smelled deliciously of cream soda and cocoa, was reading the paper. My mother came waltzing down the stairs wearing a white feather boa around her neck and a red-sequined evening gown.

We all watched her as she slithered toward the piano and slid her slim red bottom onto the black bench. She began to play a waltz that we had all heard her play a thousand times. But this time she sang to the music in a fine, high, sweet voice:

> *All the world shines with a golden glow*
> *Because you love me,*
> *And the very clouds are bowing low*
> *Because you love me,*
> *Every little flower, every tree,*
> *Seems to join me in my ecstasy,*
> *Because you've told them I'm the one,*
> *I'm the one, alone.*
>
> *The moon is beaming down on us tonight*
> *Because you love me,*
> *The stars are dancing in its silvery light*
> *Because you love me,*

The heavens and the earth
Smile and rejoice,
The bells ring out in lilting happy voice,
Because you've told them I'm your choice,
I'm your choice alone.

She swayed back and forth on the piano bench, the low-cut gown exposing the delicate bones of her spine. I had never seen her in that red dress before. She made the piano sing as I never could when I banged out my Bach inventions and my Bartok exercises. My father stared in admiration. My Aunt Hilda's mouth was a thin line.

39

"I'm sending this song in to a contest," my mother announced when she had played the last triumphant chords. "I heard about it on the radio. If they choose my song, they will send me and my family out to Hollywood, California."

My father, looking worshipful, applauded loudly with his big powerful hands. Upstairs, my little sister started to scream from her crib. My mother had high color on her face; she was radiant with excitement.

"*Then* we'll move," my mother announced to my Aunt Hilda. I laid my head down in Aunt Hilda's lap, and she stroked my hair gently.

"Go up, Hilda," my grandmother said, "and get the baby quiet."

"*I'll* go up," my mother said.

"Let Hilda go," my grandmother said. "She's the only one who knows how to soothe her."

Aunt Hilda sat paralyzed, holding me. My mother tossed her feather boa and smiled. She went upstairs, her hips swinging, to quiet the baby.

The next morning I was chosen to be the one to mail off my mother's song and my father's proposal letter to Sears. I walked proudly to the mailbox on the corner and pulled open the metal door. Making sure no one was looking, I quickly kissed both envelopes and dropped them into the mailbox, together, one on top of the other.

When I got back to the house, I found my mother and Aunt Hilda sitting together at the kitchen table, their faces frozen. They had just learned, from a neighbor's phone call, that Harriet had caught polio. Her first symptom had been the dreaded stiff neck. She was in the hospital, burning with a high fever.

We waited all day for news. Toward evening we learned that Harriet's legs had become paralyzed. Very late that night my friend died. The next day Mrs. Gargano went **40** from house to house so that everyone in our Girl Scout troop could sign a sympathy card addressed to Harriet's parents. I wasn't allowed to sign it—my mother said she didn't want me touching a card everyone else had touched.

She kept me in the house for the rest of the summer, watching me all the time. She and Aunt Hilda whispered together, thinking up ways to entertain me so I would not try to go out in the dangerous air on the stoop, or play jacks in the alley, or attempt Russian Seven with my pink Spalding ball against the brick wall of the house next-door.

When the summer ended, my mother reluctantly allowed me to go back to school, but each day when I came home she felt my forehead anxiously and asked me if I could bend my neck forward. Just after Christmas, a man who collected statues of elephants came into the antique store and priced the most impressive and valuable object my father owned. It stood in the window on a red velvet cloth—a four-foot-tall bronze elephant with a gleaming ruby in its forehead and real ivory tusks. When my father learned that the man was a carpenter, a trade was arranged—the elephant in exchange for the conversion of our one-family house to a two-family house. By springtime, my Aunt Hilda and my grandmother had moved upstairs into their own apartment, which had a specially built bathroom sink in it designed for giving shampoos. The staircase between the upstairs and downstairs now had doors with locks at both ends. The closed-in sunporch became the bedroom my sister and I had to share. Each morning the sun exploded through its nine windows, shocking us awake.

TABU

. . . .

Although Mrs. Marcus frequently came across the street to our house saying she needed to borrow sugar or margarine, I knew she really came to report to my mother on the progress of Ruthie's freakish chest development. First she would sigh with exasperation. "Can you imagine? I have to *shlep* all the way downtown to Macy's again to get her another brassiere. That child grows a cup size every week!" Another sigh, barely concealing her proud astonishment. Then a sideways glance at me, having my milk and cookies at the kitchen table.

My mother didn't have to look at me. She knew every inch of me. When I looked at her, there was no mistaking the mortification on her face: we came from a family of flat-chested women. I could tell she was thinking that if evolution continued on its present course, women like us would soon be extinct.

My father, sensitive to the leaden gloom left behind in the wake of one of these visits, was hard-pressed to know just how to comfort me. He reminded me that I was still the champion jacks player on our block—a position Ruthie had aspired to since fourth grade. He suggested I might even have hidden talents I hadn't fully explored. My long, dextrous fingers, for example. Would it not be wise for me to resume piano lessons again? When I showed no gratitude, he added, puffing on his pipe, letting out clouds of butterscotch-scented smoke, "You do know, I hope, that you have lovely hair."

Lovely hair! I had wild curls which popped out each morning from my scalp like powerful springs! (Ruthie had straight black shining hair, which hung down her back like a curtain. Her mother once said to mine, "I think a Chinaman must have crept through my window one night!" My mother had replied, "Knowing you, I can believe it!")

Claus Mueller, the third of my many piano teachers, was hired that winter. This time I promised to apply myself. It was becoming evident, now that I was soon to turn fourteen, that I had better look to my future in earnest. I acknowledged to myself with regret that great beauty would not be my forte; therefore other avenues had to be developed . . . quickly! As if it were not absolutely evident, my mother pointed out to me that Claus Mueller, who would be coming weekly to the house to instruct me, was a *man*. This in itself suggested the importance of my talent, as nearly all my friends took piano lessons from women. Mr. Mueller, a bachelor of about thirty, was six feet four inches tall. During my lessons, as I played and replayed the measures he requested, he paced back and forth through our living room wearing his overcoat and a long wool muffler. He tossed his turbulent, bushy hair and signaled his approval of a well-done passage by a snort through his large nose. At certain moments I found him to be almost handsome. To distract myself from the endless repetition of scales which he required of me, I imagined the ad for Tabu—imagined my mother ceasing her endless pairing of socks on the couch, imagined her going down to the basement to stare at the clothes revolving in the Bendix, imagined Mr. Mueller unwrapping his long muffler and lassoing my shoulders with it, imagined him sliding me off the smooth black piano bench and into his arms, where he would kiss me with the passion of a Beethoven gone wild.

Ruthie also started taking lessons from him. Her mother had the eye of a buzzard when it came to Ruthie's advancement; Mrs. Marcus told my mother she felt Ruthie needed

44

to develop some ladylike skills, which I thought was a laugh. I feared her fingers might become so strengthened by playing scales that she'd eventually be able to bypass me in "eightsies" at jacks. In truth, she'd stopped playing jacks with me at the end of last summer, never being able to get much past "fivesies." Thinking of Claus Mueller pacing in Ruthie's living room gave me grief. Knowing Ruthie, her craftiness, and the way she could pop out with new talents, I worried that she might emerge as the next José Iturbi.

We were in the first year of high school that winter. Ruthie had begun traveling with a different crowd. Dark, handsome Italian boys, who wore the top three buttons of their shirts undone and sported large crucifixes which gleamed aggressively from the swirls of their black chest hair, circled about her in the lunchroom. As if witnessing a miracle, they hopped about and genuflected as she delicately dipped potato chips into a swirl of mustard which she had dabbed onto the center of the cellophane bag. Potato chips and mustard—I, too, was awed by so inspired an innovation. Each day I dutifully ate a tuna salad sandwich and an overripe banana for my lunch. Ruthie began wearing the collar of her blouse turned up in back—but always was careful to smooth it down on the bus on the way home after school.

I continued to associate with my old friends from grammar school—whiny girls with thick ankles who aspired to gain ever more badges to sew on their Girl Scout uniforms. Some of them were also scheduled to give piano recitals which I was obliged to attend. At these performances my friends wore starched cotton dresses with puffed sleeves. I thanked heaven that Claus Mueller had not once suggested a recital might be looming in the future for me.

In theory, Ruthie was still in my Girl Scout troop, but she rarely came to meetings. During the last meeting she attended, we were shown a film on menstruation. On the screen little butterflies circled around a flower while a sugary voice told us that with proper hygiene, no would ever know we were having our "delicate condition."

"That's not true," Ruthie announced. "I smell different then, even to myself." We all stared at her, astonished at the implications of her knowledge, her crudity, her daring.

Mrs. Marcus continued to borrow sugar and margarine from my mother, but the news about her trips to Macy's was no longer so remarkable; Ruthie apparently had reached her upper limit, a C cup, and Mrs. Marcus could only announce, when she felt the need to use impressive numbers, how many (and not how big) were the brassieres she had to buy for her daughter.

"Practice your scales!" my mother urged me as the afternoons turned dark early. She buttoned her sweater against the chill. "I hear that Ruthie is up to 'Für Elise' already."

I shrugged. I was doing the sonatinas of Diabelli. I was doing *theory* in my music notebook. "Für Elise" was like onesies in jacks.

News of the party came from my mother, not from Ruthie. "We have to get you a pretty new dress," my mother announced one evening, as she was frying liver on the stove. I noticed how shapeless her housedress was; I realized that my lack of style was largely due to her insufficiencies.

"What for?" I was really most interested in my father's big shirts these days; I wore them over my dungarees and they hid the exact size of my chest. No one seeing me in one of his shirts could know if I was an A, a B, or a C.

"So you'll look nice for Ruthie's party."

"What party?"

"Her birthday party."

"When is it?"

"You know when her birthday is. January 12."

"She didn't mention any party to me."

"Well, you'll be getting an invitation, don't worry."

"Ruthie and I hardly talk to each other anymore."

"Well, you've been friends for years. Her mother says Ruthie wouldn't *dream* of having a party without inviting you." When she saw the look on my face, she added, "Besides, you don't have all that many parties to go to these days, do you?"

Invitations to two major events came in one day's mail. One was to Ruthie's party:

> *We're having a little shindig,*
> *The donkey's on the wall—*
> *The dartboard's on the table,*
> *We're going to have a ball!*

47

The other was to a fashion show at Abraham and Straus department store:

> *Dear Scout Family,*
> *Girl Scout Troop #383 is proud to an-*
> *nounce their participation in a fashion*
> *show of spring and summer delights, all*
> *modeled by our own scouts. Each girl will*
> *model the fashion best suited to her looks,*
> *and best news of all—each girl will get a 50*
> *percent discount to buy the outfit she mod-*
> *els! Don't miss it! See you there!"*

"I'm not a model," I told my mother at once. "My leaders didn't even ask my permission for this."

"No one else is a model either," my mother said. "You'll do it; you'll see, you'll have fun, you'll get a party dress at half-price just in time for Ruthie's party. You can surprise her in a beautiful new dress."

"Ruthie's in my troop, Ma. She'll get this letter. She'll probably get a new dress too."

"She won't come," my mother predicted. "Mrs. Marcus says Ruthie's way beyond Girl Scouts. She's a law unto herself."

A week before Ruthie's party, on the day of the fashion show, we bumped into Ruthie and her mother on the platform of the Avenue N train station. Snow was just beginning to fall. I was wearing a storm coat, a woolen stocking cap, and gloves.

"You're going downtown?" my mother asked.

"None other," Mrs. Marcus said.

48 Ruthie stood on the far side of her mother. Melting snowflakes were beginning to glitter like drops of mercury in the filaments of her black hair. She wore a sailor's pea jacket, the kind worn only by the tough girls at our high school.

"Ruthie is modeling?" my mother asked.

"She is."

"For the discount?"

"For the career experience," Mrs. Marcus said.

"She's going to be a *model?*" my mother asked, turning toward Ruthie.

Ruthie performed for my mother a little smirk she had been perfecting at school, a maneuver during which she made her red mouth into a tight line and flipped up the corners of her lips briefly.

"Just think of it," my mother said dreamily. "From the same block, two famous girls, friends since childhood. A beautiful model and a concert pianist."

Ruthie had walked away from us to study two dirty words written in black crayon on a Tabu ad. When the train came, we took seats—I with my mother, she with hers, we behind them. Once we were underground, rushing through the great subterranean tunnels, the evocative words bounced in front of my eyes each time the bulbs in the ceiling of the car dimmed or flickered out entirely.

The mothers sat in a small auditorium, and our Girl
Scout leaders and the girls from my troop milled around in
a tiny, freezing dressing room. An officious woman, wearing
a pencil behind her ear, told us to strip down to our slips.
The command in itself was an alarming challenge. Without
storm coats, loose cotton dresses, big shirts belonging to
our fathers, it was all out there for everyone to see; right
under the slip—the bra and its obvious size: measure of our
future happiness, indicator of our fortunes in the years to
come.

The bossy woman slapped a tape measure around my
chest, my waist, my hips. "30, 22, 30," she called out.
"This one is hopeless."

Hopeless!

Suddenly, I missed my father desperately. *Daddy,* I im-
plored him, *what about my pretty hair? What about my
dexterity at Diabelli sonatinas? Did my talents at jacks, my
good grades count for nothing?*

An intake of breath from my fellow scouts caused me to
look over my shoulder. Ruthie was emerging from behind a
screen wearing the first bikini I had ever seen in person. I
experienced a physical stab of pain in my throat, in my
chest. Her breasts, which heretofore had been fabulous,
were made real. Soft, velvety, creamy, they shimmered,
they quivered. They protruded from her basic body in a
way that seemed dangerous, fantastic, diabolical. I suddenly knew why males must adore her, why the young
Italians circled her in the lunch room, why the neighborhood boys gathered on her stoop after school and
begged her to come out and play stoop ball with them. I
recognized with a fatalistic grief that, by nature of my sex, I
was not destined to relish those unique extrusions personally, but at least I should *have* them!

The girls fluttered around Ruthie like the butterflies
around the flower in the menstruation film. Her measurements were called out, announced, exclaimed over. Her

49

little pink bikini glowed like the sun. "This one will sell like hotcakes," the officious woman announced. "For you, hon, you don't get 50 percent off, you get to keep it free."

"Free! Free!" Ruthie ran out to the stage of the auditorium and called the news down to her mother. I knew my mother was waiting for *my* news. Waiting to see *my* act.

On me they tried outfit after outfit. Time was getting short. Guests were arriving to fill the auditorium. A middy-blouse and skirt were lowered over my head, then a shirt-waist dress, then a circle skirt with a poodle embroidered on it, with matching sweater and scarf.

50   "Everything hangs on this one," the woman said. "Too bad we don't have a shower curtain for her to model."

I stood there, once again in my slip, glaring at her. She said loudly, in her cigarette-hoarse voice, "Sorry, we can't use you, kiddo, so you might as well go down and watch the show." When she turned her back, I took a straight pin out of a pin cushion I saw on a chair and stuck it in the seat of her dress, straight in. One of these hours she was going to have to sit down.

There was a blizzard the night of Ruthie's party. Looking out my kitchen window at the black, freezing sky, I announced that I didn't think I would go.

"You have to, it's an obligation," my mother said. We had worked out some weird outfit—a gabardine skirt, borrowed from my aunt, pinned to fit at the waist; a blouse with gardenias on it, which my mother had worn on her honeymoon. Patent leather flats, real stockings, a garter belt that was killing me. Around my neck on a black velvet ribbon was my grandmother's cameo: it had the profile of a queenly woman on one side and lilies of the valley hand-painted on the other. Set in gold. Surrounded by seed pearls. The family heirloom. My mother dabbed perfume on my throat and behind my ears. I felt her linger, looking behind my ears to see if they were clean. If she had dared to

say one word, I would have burst into tears, but she didn't.
She just kissed my forehead and said, "Do you want Daddy
to walk you over?"

"No," I said, but my father put his pipe down in a saucer
on the kitchen table and began pulling on his galoshes.

"It's only across the street," I insisted.

"It's icy out there," my father said.

"It's dark," my mother warned.

"It's dangerous," my father added.

"I've crossed that street a million times."

"Not in a terrible storm."

I put on my storm coat. My mother had offered to lend   **51**
me her skunk fur coat, perhaps to make up for the fact that
I didn't get a new dress at half-price, but I declined,
believing privately that it still smelled of skunk.

Once we were outside, my father took my elbow and
guided me down the iced-over front steps. From there he
walked ahead of me through the deepening snowdrifts.

"Step in my footsteps so you don't get your feet wet," he
said. I tiptoed after him, my small feet fitting neatly in the
outline of his huge ones. In the street, the snow was ridged
in strange patterns by the tires of cars; I could see diamond
shapes and parallel lines in the faint light coming from
Ruthie's windows. I had made this trip to her house at *least*
a million times: to play jacks, to have lunch, to run with her
under the sprinkler, to pick cherries from the tree in her
backyard, to sleep over, to play house.

My father waited while I rang the bell. He stood hunched
in the cold wind, his coat open at the neck. I wondered why
I had never bought him a muffler. I began to worry about
his exposed throat. For the first time I thought that perhaps
he could someday get sick, catch pneumonia, even die.

Finally we heard footsteps coming down the hall. My
father bent and kissed the top of my head. "Call me when
you're ready to come home."

"What if it's late?"

"Call me. It's just across the street. No trouble. It's slippery crossing alone."

He left me there, to cross alone himself. Mrs. Marcus opened the door wearing her coat, with Mr. Marcus all bundled up right behind her. "Come right in," Ruthie's mother said. "You kids will have all the privacy you need. Ruthie made us agree to go to the movies. She promised to be a little angel without us here—Scout's honor."

The door closed behind me like the gate of a prison. I adjusted the cameo around my neck and walked forward.

52   Five Italian boys I recognized from the lunchroom at school were there in Ruthie's living room, slouched on the couch and slumped in the two armchairs. They looked as if they didn't belong on furniture, but should instead be on leashes or in cages. Some girl I didn't know—she was dressed in the mode of a Spanish flamenco dancer—was playing "Chopsticks" very badly on the piano. She had a broken comb sticking out of her hair like a chicken bone.

"Hi," I greeted them because—before I had left the house—my mother had advised me that it never hurt to be friendly. I scanned the sunporch for signs of another familiar soul—praying for even a girl from my Girl Scout troop. *Where was the donkey? Where was the dartboard?* "Where's Ruthie?" I said finally, into the air. Then I stared at my feet. The glare from my patent leather shoes nearly blinded me.

"Getting ready," one of the animals on the couch growled mysteriously. He was chewing on a toothpick. I seriously doubted that his father had crossed any streets to get *him* here.

"I'll go get ready, too," the Spanish dancer said, and, with a little spin of her red gauzy skirt, she disappeared.

After a moment, I sat down primly on the piano bench, my back to the keys.

"You gonna give us a concert?" asked the one with the toothpick.

"Maybe Ruthie will, a little later," I suggested. "I'm told she's doing very well on 'Für Elise.' And this *is* her party."

"A concert isn't what she's planning to give, you can be sure of that," he said. They all laughed very hard at this, and when the laughter died down, one of them started it up again, as if he were revving a motor in his throat. They kept this up, sounding like a herd of motorcycles. I stood up finally and chose a pretzel from a bowl on the table.

"Who are *you?*" one of them finally said to me. "You look like you wandered in here by mistake."

"I'm Lady Godiva!" I said nastily, shocking myself. "Who do I look like?"

At last Ruthie made her entrance, flanked by the Spanish dancer and three girls I recognized from my gym class as ones who were always getting detention notices. She sashayed in wearing a pink cashmere sweater which was decorated, on the rise of one of her extraordinary breasts, with a plastic pin shaped like a telephone. Ruthie's phone number was inscribed in the center of the dial in large black letters. She wore a black straight skirt, slit high at the sides. And she wore real high heels, sling backs, black suede, with little rhinestones set in a design at the toe. She glanced at me as if she had never seen me before and had no idea why I might be there.

"Happy birthday," I said, finally.

She ignored me. "We're ready," she announced to the boys.

"For what?" I asked.

"It's a party game," she said impatiently, shaking one shoulder as if an annoying fly had landed on it. Then the creatures lumbered off the couch and chairs and all nine of them disappeared into Ruthie's bedroom.

Ruthie's bedroom! Whose door they now closed in my face as I tried to follow them in! The room where we had played with our Sparkle Plenty dolls together, had scraped the polished floorboards raw with the metal spikes of our jacks.

I went back to the room and was alone so long I ate all the pretzels in the bowl. Then I started on the M&Ms. I was beginning to feel nauseated. I considered that they might be playing a game where I was "it"—as in hide-and-seek—and expected me to go after them and find them. But it didn't seem likely; by now I felt they would have called me if that were the case.

I looked for the pile of comic books Ruthie used to keep on a shelf under the coffee table, but all I found there was a *True Romance* which had on its cover a photograph of a woman wearing a slip with one strap torn. She was turning her head away from a man who was shouting at her.

For some reason, I began to wish Claus Mueller were here, seeing me all dressed up, sitting alone in Ruthie's living room while the party went on behind her closed bedroom door. I thought he should know about the way she was treating me, but it was not something I could ever tell him while I was taking a piano lesson; certainly not while my mother sat on the couch listening, darning my father's socks or folding laundry. I thought I might write Claus Mueller a letter and leave it, sealed and addressed to him, in Ruthie's *Classical Easy Favorites for Beginning Piano* book.

Having nothing else to do, I spread out my aunt's skirt on Ruthie's piano bench, changed the position of my cameo so it did not close off my windpipe, and commenced to play through the classical easy favorites, one after another. I was on "Country Gardens," conjuring at just what note, should I be giving Claus Mueller a private concert, he might slide me off the bench with his muffler and fold me in his arms,

54

when I felt a flare of anger ride up me like an army of poisonous bugs.

I jumped off the bench and stomped to Ruthie's bedroom where I pounded very hard on the door.

"Who is it?" grunted one of the hulks, whose job, it seemed, was guard dog.

"Lady Godiva," I said. "What's going on in there?"

"That's for us to know and you to find out."

I banged on the door again. I heard a low rumble of laughter. Then mumblings, whisperings, a quick debate. I heard Ruthie's voice say "No! If my mother finds out . . ."

I examined the poster on Ruthie's door: Alice-in-Won-   **55** derland beginning to fade through the looking glass. I stroked the lines of Alice's hair and waited. The door opened a crack, then closed again. Ruthie's voice: "We have to let her in or my mother will kill me." Another long conference.

Why didn't I just leave? I didn't want to be here, did I? Then why did I so desire to set my patent leather shoes inside that room?

The door swung open. The guard dog stepped back. "You can come in now," he said. His crucifix swung as he bowed, mocking me, to invite me in. I stepped into the room, dimly illuminated by Ruthie's Mickey Mouse night-lamp. Mickey, with his white-gloved fingers held up in the air like fat white sausages, looked to me like a lunatic.

I entered further. A rank smell in the cave-like room seemed compounded of sweat, perfume, and rancid Pixie Pink lipstick. Ruthie—from a darkened corner—said to me, "You can play one round with us. You take my place."

"How do I play?" I asked. "What are the rules?" I had a fleeting thought that I could still get out.

"Do what you're told," Ruthie's voice—sinister, almost unrecognizable—instructed me. Just then one of the girls took my arm and pulled me over toward Ruthie's bed. I was

positioned along its long edge and other girls were pushed
into place on either side of me. I could feel the flounce of
Ruthie's quilt against the back of my legs. I had always
admired the flying unicorns on her quilt. The one on my
bed had teddy bears on it.

"The rules are simple," Ruthie said. "When the Mickey
Mouse light goes out, the boys kiss the girls. That's all."

I could discern some hulking forms across the room, each
one with a foot forward, like runners about to begin a race.

"Here goes," Ruthie said. "One, two, three—GO!" The
room went black. Huge shapes catapulted out of the
darkness. One fell on me, throwing me across the width of
Ruthie's bed. On either side of me I could feel the roiling,
wrestling forms of others. A heavy, gasping face smeared
saliva across my lips. A body ground me down, screwing me
into the bed till I stopped breathing. A clawlike hand was
squeezing around among the gardenias of my chest. When a
tongue forced its way between my lips, I flung up my knee
with all the force I could muster.

"Shit!"

"Moron!" I shouted, shoving him off.

"Jesus!"

"What did she do?"

"Kicked me in the balls! Jesus!"

The light came on, showing me Ruthie's savage face as it
came right up against mine, almost nose-to-nose. "You said
you wanted to play, you little fool," she hissed.

"I did want to," I said.

"Now I suppose you'll run home and tell your mother."

"That's for me to know and you to find out," I said right
back to her, eyeball-to-eyeball.

The slobberer was getting up from his knees now, quickly
recovered. "You better pay up, Marcus," he said. "A deal is
a deal."

Ruthie scowled. "Okay," she said. "Get in the closet with

me, right now." She followed him in; I heard her skate key
fall off its hook and hit the floor.

"You can let me out of here now," I said to the guard dog,
who was sitting on the floor beside the door. Sullenly he
flicked it open.

"Lady Godiva," he said. "Who the hell is that?"

"*You'd* never know in a million years," I said.

"At least I'd never've sold out," he sneered. "Kiss you?
Never! Not even to feel Marcus up."

"Down, boy," I said. "Chew on your bone."

Before I got my storm coat from the hall closet, I tore the
Alice-in-Wonderland poster off Ruthie's door, letting it keel
over onto the floor. Then, buttoning all my buttons, I went
to stand at a window in Ruthie's sunporch, debating
whether or not to call my father. I stared across Avenue O
at my house.

The snow was still falling, falling softly, cushioning the
points of the hedges, blunting the sharp edges of steps,
stoops, sills. My house looked like a dollhouse—tiny, re-
mote, the square bright windows quartered by the window
supports. Shadows passed across the yellow squares: my
mother, my father, doing their nightly dance, crossing,
turning, moving, as if they had no awareness of the thrilling
dramas being played out in the world just beyond the thin
cold panes of glass.

The black street looked like a chasm. I let myself out into
the snow. I examined the snowdrifts to see if I could locate
my father's footsteps, but they were long gone. Although the
street seemed endless, slippery, vast, I made my way, slip-
ping, skimming, almost skating over the icy plain. I grasped
the brass handle of my front door with pleasure and hung
onto it for a long moment, surveying the distance I had
come. I had found the crossing quite manageable, even
agreeable.

HONEST
MISTAKES

. . . .

My mother wasn't talking to my father in Miami Beach in the summer of 1955. A man named Frank Stuart had conned my father into giving him our family's life savings: "Just for the payroll, just over the weekend, just till Monday." My father hadn't even asked my mother's permission; he couldn't conceive of dishonesty—at the very worst he believed in honest mistakes. He was still hoping it would get straightened out, that Stuart would turn up with the two thousand dollars, with an apology that he'd had to leave town for some emergency, that in fact he was back on the job in which my father was a new partner. Construction was big in Florida then. The whole world wanted to live in Florida, a paradise on earth. Hadn't we come here for that?

After a certain point, my mother did not engage in further discussion with him. In silence each morning she got dressed to leave for work: she'd had to take a job as a typist at Wimbush Realty to pay the rent. It wasn't enough—we were in trouble. My father spent the day reading the classified ads. He was still circling "Business Opportunities" in red pencil, though she'd told him, in one of their fights, to forget that crap and look for a *job*. He wanted to open his own small business—all he needed was a little capital again.

After she left, he and I were stuck together in our blistering one-bedroom, northwest-exposure apartment. (A southeast exposure got the ocean breeze—but those apartments cost *money*.) Slouched on the studio couch where he slept (my mother slept on the other one, catty-cornered),

running his fingers through his wild, curly hair, he smiled
at me from time to time, just a shadow of his old, sweet,
reassuring smile, but I couldn't buy it. I was having problems of my own: a new high school, a new climate, and,
worst of all, Lilijoy, a girl from my school who lived in the
apartment right above ours and had boys honking for her
at all hours from fancy convertibles (visible—if I *looked*—
from my bedroom window).

"I'm going to think about a job, Daddy," I said to him
one morning. "There's too much time on my hands." I lifted
a section of the classifieds from his lap—and I got my own
red pencil. My parents didn't expect me to get a summer
job; boys got jobs. Boys had to buy gas for their cars and
take girls out on dates, so boys got beachboy jobs at hotel
pools, putting out towels, arranging cushions on chaise
lounges, and catering, in general, to the wealthy women
who rented cabanas. Once in a while a girl from school
would invite me to her cabana, where we would change into
bathing suits and then swim in the hotel pool. Most of the
girls in my class were from rich families who owned houses
on Indian Creek Drive or Alton Road and whose mothers
kept cabanas. The others were like me, squashed into one-
or two-bedroom apartments near the high school or in
North Beach while their fathers tested the various business
angles of paradise.

A stifling humid puff of air, sifting around the corner of
the building, ruffled the pages of the newspaper. I had had
my own dreams of paradise, hatched and embellished on
the three-day-long car journey last fall from Brooklyn to
Miami Beach. With a U-Haul trailer bouncing about behind
us, my father, in high spirits, draped a towel on his head
like an Arab and occasionally hooted like an Indian. I
preferred to lay low in the backseat and think my own
thoughts. I imagined myself, for one thing, wearing an aqua
linen dress on the first day of school—it would complement
my gorgeous suntan-to-be. I also imagined that we would

60

live in a perky little house under a row of palm trees near
the beach; it would have a hedge around it. On the other
side of the hedge would be another house in which a handsome boy lived. I would walk through the hedge in my linen
dress and sit with him on his front step. He would give me a
coconut. That was as far as the fantasy went, but it was
quite enough to set my heart pounding with hope.

From upstairs now, I could hear Lilijoy laughing in the
hallway, then the thud of loud footsteps on the stairs, the
slam of the outside door, the roar of a boy's car.

My father and I looked at each other. He knew. He raised
his eyebrows at me and went back to the paper. We couldn't   **61**
really help each other. I circled an ad: "Doctor's Assistant,
No Experience Needed."

After my interview with Dr. Zucker, I went to a thrift
shop in South Beach and bought a nurse's uniform. It was
100 percent nylon and zipped up the back, a little tight for
me. The zipper pulled in my waist dramatically before the
cascade of gathered pleats and big pockets fell over my
hips. Nylon was hot in the Miami Beach sun, and I had to
wait a long time on Lincoln Road for my bus home, but I
felt happy. I had just got a job on the first try, and I had
bumped into Roger Slavitt in front of Walgreen's and he'd
asked me if I could spare some time to tutor him in English;
he was a football player who had been on the front page of
the *Beachcomber* every week during the schoolyear. *Slavitt
Scores Winning Touchdown. Slavitt Escorts Homecoming
Queen to Prom.* We'd arrranged that he'd come over next
Saturday afternoon and I'd explain Emily Dickinson to
him. I wasn't wearing aqua linen when he saw me, but white
nylon, and the effect, I felt, was dazzling. I thought, in fact,
I looked a little like a bride.

The job promised to be easy. Dr. Zucker had two offices;
while he was in the Miami office, I was to man the phones in

the Miami Beach office and make appointments. When he
was present, I was to funnel the patients into the examining
rooms, set out the injection bottles, and later autoclave the
syringes. He had outlined a few other duties: sorting sample medicines, ordering bottles of liver extract when they
got low, sweeping the floor, wiping down the sinks, typing a
few invoices. I had the feeling that he hadn't even looked at
me during the interview. My impression of him was of a tall
black-haired old man with a pencil-thin mustache.

From the window of the reception area, I could see down
to the end of Lincoln Road to the ocean. The blur of blue
sky blending into blue sea gave me a sense that the world
was pillowed in a spongy, protective cushion. Being high
up—the twelfth floor—made me feel powerful; the cold
blast of the air conditioning was bracing. I was certainly
much better off here than sitting in our apartment, glumly
commiserating with my father. On my desk was *The Taming
of the Shrew*. It was slow going, but I intended to better
myself over the summer, which my mother thought was
essential for me to do. She had assured me that I'd worked
hard all year and deserved the summer to rest and read and
get smart.

"Are you college-bound?" Dr. Zucker had asked me. "Or
can I count on you to stay on here?"

"I can't possibly afford to go to college," I told him. "My
father lost his fortune in a business investment. I have to
help the family out. I think you should consider me a
permanent employee." Dr. Zucker seemed to understand I
had already graduated from high school. I let it stand. I
feared that I might actually *not* be able to go back to high
school—that I would keep this job forever, sitting on my
reclining desk chair and looking out over the ocean.

The first two women who came for their appointments
carried Saks purses and wore big diamonds on their fingers. Gold pendants hung around their sunburn-scorched,
wrinkled necks. I realized very soon that all Dr. Zucker's

62

patients were old; this surprised me because the sign on his
door said he was a gynecologist. I'd had the idea the office
would be full of pregnant women radiant with the glow of
impending motherhood. Instead, his patients were fading
and fairly desperate about it.

A few times Dr. Zucker warned me not to forget to put the
liver extract back in the refrigerator or it would lose its
potency. Occasionally he left it out overnight himself, then
injected it into the ladies anyway. Once, when I began to tell
him the extract was warm and useless, he winked at me,
and I shut my mouth. Later I asked him what the liver
extract was supposed to do, and he said, "It's the fountain   **63**
of youth, honey," and he winked at me again.

While he was in his Miami office, two mornings a week, I
passed the time by reading his medical texts. The pictures
of diseased female genitalia caused my heart to skip beats;
they were grossly magnified and no human connection was
visible; just swollen parts, with tumors, or suppurating
sores, or orifices with speculums inserted in them. Occasionally I felt I must have some air, but Dr. Zucker had
warned me never to open the windows; the building was old
and the frames were rusted shut from the salt air.

Sometimes I browsed through his files of medical charts,
but they were full of technical language, and his handwrit-
ing was difficult to decipher. I spun on my chair. I typed a
few bills. I read a little Shakespeare. I daydreamed about
Roger Slavitt. He was coming to my house every Saturday.
Mr. Katz, our principal, had warned him that if he didn't
improve his English grade, he would be forbidden to play
on the team in his senior year.

Roger and I didn't stay two minutes in the apartment; the
air was sour with hostility between my parents, who were
still not speaking. Since the bedroom had been graciously
assigned to me, my mother and father were careful to
occupy only the living room, sitting on their respective

studio couches unless my mother was silently making my father a meal. He hadn't yet "forgotten that crap" and found a job though he pretended to be looking for the right one. The truth was that he cruised around Miami Beach construction sites looking for Frank Stuart, bearing him no particular malice. He simply hoped he was back in business, and they could go on from where they had left off—with that promising deal.

64 Roger, who stood six foot four in his huge white sneakers, was disturbing to my mother. She had to support the back of her head with her hand in order to look up at him. While I was getting my books together, my father told Roger he was thinking about "going into upholstery on a shoestring—all you need are some tacks and a roll of cloth." Roger told my father that sounded good to him, that his father had started out in the used furniture business and now owned three factories. Then he smiled at my mother. She didn't respond. She had actually turned white-haired in the last months. She was working overtime for Wimbush Realty, where properties were sold for enormous profits while she was being paid a typist's wage. To cheer her up, and because I felt nervous about walking out the door with Roger, I whispered to her as we left that we ought to have lunch out together on Monday. She agreed it would be fun—but said she'd bring along a picnic and we could eat in the doctor's office. It would be cheaper.

Roger and I walked across the street to a little kids' playground, and I let him choose a bench. He wanted to keep his suntan, so I said I didn't mind sweating it out. The sun, coming off his white T-shirt and shorts, created dancing stars in my eyes. I handed him the book and told him to ask me about the things he didn't understand. He wanted to know why hope was the thing with feathers. He said how come the day undressed herself and wore gold garters. He

said how come, if Emily was nobody, and she said so
herself, we had to read her poetry.

I told him "There is no Frigate like a Book to take us
Lands away," and he said, "Friggin' books," and laughed. I
wanted to keep him there as long as I could. I hoped Lilijoy
would come bounding down the stairs and out the door and
see us sitting there on the bench: the big football player and
me. I wanted to stay a long time watching the sun bead the
perspiration on the golden hairs of Roger's thighs. Anything
was better than going back into the apartment to sit there in
the thick animosity of my parents' bitterness. Why was I so
stuck? There were things going on in the world to which I
had no access at all: parties, movies, pizza outings, night-
time barbecues at the beach. Roger talked about these
things as if they were the stuff of life itself. He was dating
Penny Bloom, the homecoming queen. He told me he loved
to take her to Fun Fair, the hot-dog place on the causeway,
where you could put anything on your hot dog for free,
onions, pickles, ketchup, mustard, sauerkraut, and then
play miniature golf till they closed down. After that, he'd
drive only with Penny to Pelican's Island, where they'd
"you-know-what" till the police swept the place with their
flashlights. "God, me and Penny are so frustrated, if you
know what I mean," Roger confided in me. "And the last
thing we need is Trouble." He rolled his eyes. "Like
Brenda." Brenda was the girl whose father caught her in
the shower with her boyfriend and a few weeks later she
turned out to be pregnant in the bargain. I looked over the
playground to where some kids were on a jungle gym.

"Hey, did I insult you?" Roger said. "I didn't mean to
talk dirty or off-color or anything. Listen—I never even
asked you, what are *you* doing for fun this summer?"

"I'm working for a gynecologist," I said.

Suddenly he peered at me. I noticed that his face was
enormous. He had very large slug-like lips, one on top of

65

the other, like nesting primitive animals. They looked truly bizarre to me.

"Hey, you wouldn't be able to get hold of any stuff, would you, I mean, you know, one of those things, to prevent trouble like Brenda had?"

"One of what things?" I said, though I knew immediately what he meant.

"The thing the woman wears. You know? Penny says she can't get one unless she goes to a doctor and tells him she's getting married."

"I might be able to get you one," I told Roger. "The doctor has them in his office."

"Oh, if only you could get me one!" Roger said. "I mean get Penny one. I'd do anything for you! What do you want me to do for you?"

"Let's just go sit on the steps of my apartment building," I told him. "Or, better yet, could we sit in your car in front of my house?"

"Sure," he said. "But I don't get it."

"That's okay," I said. "You don't have to."

He had a two-tone blue Chevrolet, and I fiddled with the radio till "Hold Me, Thrill Me, Kiss Me" came blasting out. After a while Lilijoy came to her window and flashed her head back and forth, two or three times. Finally I knew she had seen us and taken it in. I went right on reading to Roger:

> *The Dying need but little, Dear,*
> *A Glass of Water's All . . .*

On Monday morning, Dr. Zucker was standing at the instrument table, looking in the mirror above it and trimming his mustache with scissors I had taken from the autoclave a few minutes before. When he was done, he laid the scissors back in place in the cabinet. No appointments were scheduled for this morning and only one patient was expected after lunch—Mrs. Greenbaum. Dr. Zucker stood looking out the window and talked to me. He confided that because things were slow he had been advised by a colleague about a new idea for business. He wanted me to do a little job for him this morning: would I mind taking a packet of special business cards around to a few nearby hotels. He held one out for me to examine. It showed the snakes of the caduceus wound around its winged staff and read: *Dr. Sidney Zucker, Specialist in Honeymoon Disorders.* He told me he had already made an arrangement with several hotel managers. This is how it would work: If a manager noticed that a honeymoon couple was not, for example, going up to their room for their mid-afternoon nap, if it was clear that they were not holding hands across their beachchairs, then the manager would tactfully place Dr. Zucker's card on the nightstand in their room. If, as a result, the doctor got a new patient, the manager would get his cut. Dr. Zucker let his lips smile at me. He reminded me of Roger, who had also asked me to do him a strange favor. "Vaginismus is common," he added. "It generally scares them to death." He smiled again. "By the way, I can't be here this afternoon. When Mrs. Greenbaum comes by for her liver injection, will you give it to her?"

"Me? I'm not a nurse! I can't possibly."

"There's really nothing to it," he said. "You've seen me do it dozens of times by now. Just get the air out of the needle and have her flip up her skirt."

"No! No!" I could think of no other word to say.

"Well, don't get all excited. You can decide when she comes. For now, just lock up the office, jump on a bus, and go uptown to a few of the hotels on this list."

Dr. Zucker reached into his pocket and pulled out some change and a five-dollar bill. "Bus fare. And treat yourself to lunch, Jenny," he said. "You deserve a little bonus."

The Fountainebleau Hotel had terrazzo tile floors, sparkling with bits of marble. No one in my family had ever stayed in a hotel like this. I wandered through the lobby and then went into the coffee shop. The tinkle of silverware and glasses gave me the impression that we were all inside a music box. Everything was pink formica. Glancing at the menu, I considered bringing my mother back here to treat her to lunch with Dr. Zucker's five dollars. But the prices made my heart pound, something like the way it pounded when I examined the doctor's medical texts. To consider paying that much for a sandwich! Yet people did it. The place was full of people doing it right now! What if *I* did?

68 What if I did everything I was afraid to do? What if I did what I wanted to do, without a million considerations? Kate, the shrew, didn't worry about considerations, and she certainly had won my admiration.

I got out of there and followed the arrows to the pool where I spent a half-hour on company time admiring the muscles of the lifeguard. Women with oiled skin were turning brown on their beachchairs like chickens under the broiler. When I finally had my fill of coconut-scented suntan lotion and salty sea air, I went inside, located the manager's office, and left him a handful of the doctor's new business cards.

Back on Lincoln Road, I went straight into Dr. Zucker's private office and sat at his enormous mahogany desk. I examined photographs of his children, two sons who were surgeons somewhere in California, and one of his mother, in a babushka, taken in a village in Russia. He had had three wives, but he had no pictures displayed of any of them.

I opened his desk drawer and took out handfuls of sample medications: acne creams, dandruff shampoos, antibiotics, antihistamines, remedies for bee stings and menstrual cramps, heartburn and seasickness, sleeping pills, tranquilizers, special vitamin supplements. Many were expired, but I knew that when he gave them to patients he tore off the labels so they wouldn't know. He didn't mind my watching him do this. He liked to wink at me as if all his actions were a cause for good humor.

I chose some samples of sleeping pills and put them, as well as a good supply of other medicines, into the wide pockets of my nurse's uniform. I might need them someday. I got up from the doctor's desk and opened the storage cabinet on the wall where he kept the diaphragms. Rows of them were packed in long cardboard boxes, ranked by size (65, 70, 75, 80), and each one was in a pink vinyl kit decorated with flowers. I admired them, awed by the possible circumstances in which those springy rings encircling those powder-white rubbery cups might be brought into action. These items, too, might be expired, for all I knew. I chose a medium size for Roger, and also one for myself, along with two tubes of pearly white spermacide cream, and put them in my pockets. A pile of little booklets that explained the diaphragm's use were also for the taking, so I took two of those.

"Yoo-hoo," called a fluttery voice from down the hall, and I ran to see who it was. My nervous system was sizzling; I was not accustomed to pillaging and theft. Mrs. Greenbaum was clattering along in her lucite high heels, her blonde hair bouncing, like a separate entity, on her head. "I'm early, darling. Will you tell Doctor I have mah-jongg this afternoon, and could he do me now?"

"He's not here, Mrs. Greenbaum."

"Then you do it for me, darling. I hate to miss my shot."

"But I'm not a real nurse," I said. "I just wear this dress."

"Sweetheart, you must know how to do it! You've watched Doctor do it to me many times."

"But would you want to take a chance?" I had to know if she valued herself so lightly.

"Honey, I've taken more chances than your sweet brain

can imagine. What did my son say in the war? That he flew between the bullets? That's the story of my life."

For one second I hesitated. How did a person know in life where to draw the line? Where was it written that I had to follow all the laws? I already had stolen goods in my pockets. The liver extract bottles were *all* expired; I should tell her to go away and never come back and not waste her money. But she was reaching up to tighten a loose diamond earring: "You know—Dr. Zucker is my angel. He makes me feel like I'm eighteen every time I walk out of here. You're so lucky to work for him. He's a handsome devil, isn't he? Don't worry about it, sweetheart. I'll call and see if he can squeeze me in later in the week."

I walked her to the door and stood in the corridor till the elevator arrived. As she got into it, my mother got out, looking in her drab gray dress about fifteen years older than Mrs. Greenbaum. Maybe—I thought—I should consider giving *her* the liver extract!

She hugged me in a half-hearted way and opened her paper bag in which I saw tuna sandwiches and two prune Danishes, a special treat she bought from the Jewish bakery on Washington Avenue. She looked around and pursed her lips, letting me know she was impressed with my working conditions. She told me she worked in a room without a window and typed Wimbush's correspondence on an ancient manual machine. She'd heard—had *I* heard—about these new electric typewriters that went as fast as the wind with only a feather-touch of your fingertips. She wished that someday she could type on one of those. How nice it was to talk to my mother about something pleasant; how very nice not to have my father between us like a big sad bear.

We ate at my desk, spreading the food out on the green blotter and using the huge volume titled *Basic Gynecology Text* as a coaster for the pink and green Tupperware containers of iced tea she had brought along for us to drink.

She admired my view. I asked her if someday she would like to buy a sailboat and sail away with me to some Caribbean island.

"No men?" she asked me.

"No men," I said, and she smiled and reached over to squeeze my hand.

After lunch I showed her how I autoclaved, scrubbing the glass syringes in hot soapy water with a miniature bottle brush, wrapping the glass and the hollow needles in squares of brown linen, and then inserting them into the cavern of the silver steam oven to be sterilized.

"Maybe you should think of going to medical school," she said to me.

71

"Why bother? I could do everything right now that Dr. Zucker does, without wasting all that time and spending all that money."

I took her into one of the examining rooms; she insisted on carrying her wooden basket handbag with her everywhere in the office. I showed her where we laid the used speculums, in a glass container full of formaldehyde. One speculum was still in the sink, so I brought it over and tried to open the metal lid of the container. It was stuck. I pulled harder and suddenly the entire glass box slid off the table and crashed at my mother's feet.

She jumped away, her dress already splattered with formaldehyde. Terrible fumes rose from the floor, searing our lungs. The linoleum began to melt before our eyes.

"Oh God," I cried. We were both choking.

My mother ran to the window and tried to open it.

"Don't do that!" I yelled, but she was struggling with a rusted lever midway up the tall pane, and, when she managed to raise it, she pushed the huge window outward. We both watched the enormous rectangular frame break off at the hinges and swing out over the street as she leaned out with it, holding it by one little lever. Its bottom edge teetered on the window sill.

"Hang on to it, Ma!" I cried.

"I'm trying," she gasped, holding it now with both hands. Her bag was still swinging on her arm, a ridiculous woven basket with a stiff wooden handle and fake red cherries on the two hinged lids.

"If it drops, you'll *kill* someone!"

My mother's eyes met mine. "I didn't do it on purpose," she informed me. Her neck was taut from the effort of holding on. I couldn't help her—there was no other place to grasp the window except from the handle in her hands.

"I may have to let it go," she told me. The window was swinging in a deep, slow arc. "Look down! Is anyone on the street?"

"I can't *see* the street," I moaned, pressing my face against the other window.

"Then run outside! Go down and warn people away. I'll try to hang on as long as I can. Hurry!"

"What if you drop it before I get down?" I was begging her. "What will I do if you *kill* a person?" I was already running down the hall.

"If I do," she called back, "tell him it was just an honest mistake."

Looking up from below, on Lincoln Road, I could see the glass pane a dozen floors above me, waving like a crystal flag in the sunlight. It swung and turned, glistened and sparkled. I jumped up and down and pointed skyward, yelling at everyone on the sidewalk. "Stand back, a window is going to fall out. Get back, move away!" People glanced up and then ran into the street. A man pulled me with him and a bus thundered to a stop in order not to hit us.

Then my mother gave up the window. It fell, floating and gleaming, almost in slow motion, gyrating gently on the way down, the sky as blue as ever through its turning pane. It bounced once, like a tree, and shattered into diamonds.

I looked around. No one lay dead or bleeding. But could

I believe no damage was done? Upstairs the floor was melting away, thousands of expired pills were turning to dust,
hot air was shooting into the windowless hole and blasting
down the cold halls. Somewhere up there was my white-
haired mother, lost among the diaphragms, her basket on
her arm, as puzzled as a farm girl out to gather berries, but
not a berry anywhere.

That night, long after the sun had gone down, it appeared
my mother was still too shaken to cook. Staring at the
ceiling, she lay on her studio couch and did not protest
when I asked my father if he would take us to Fun Fair for
dinner. The lights from the lines of cars on the causeway
shimmered like a string of stars. We each ordered a mile-
long hot dog and french fries and went to the table of free
condiments to decorate our food. My father seemed to go
mad, squirting on worms of ketchup and mustard, piling
his hot dog with shards of onions and ropes of sauerkraut.
My mother put only one long line of blood-red ketchup on
her frankfurter.

We ate at an outdoor table, watching the high-school kids
and family groups playing miniature golf. Everyone was so
intense out there in the land of little castles with turrets,
and windmills, and bridges over water. People hit their golf
balls as if nothing else in the world counted. When they
missed their targets, they moaned in pain.

My father apologized to me that we weren't going to play
golf; he shrugged. It wasn't cheap to play. We could see he
was still hungry. He stood up, looked around, and went
back for more free sauerkraut, heaping it on his paper
plate in a little gray mountain.

I chewed my fried potatoes, dipping the salted zigzag
squares in ketchup, loving them and wishing there were
more.

When we finished eating (we had water to drink, Cokes
would have added another dollar to the bill), we got in the

73

car. The door on my mother's side was tied shut with rope,
so she had to slide in from my father's side, squeezing past
the steering wheel. I sat in the back.

My father, instead of going straight home to Miami
Beach, drove a short distance and then pulled off the
causeway, turning down the dirt road to Pelican's Island.

"Oh, don't go there!" I cried out as we bumped along the
rutted car tracks.

"Why not?"

I tried to think of an answer, picturing the rows of cars
with my high-school buddies in them, necking away.

74   "I need to go home and finish reading Shakespeare," I
said.

My father considered this but continued down the dirt
road. Because he had only been there before by day, to go
fishing, he seemed surprised by the astonishing population
of cars; it was like a parking lot at a drive-in movie.

I touched his shoulder. "Turn around, Daddy! Please
turn around!"

"I want to see the moon," he said. "I'm entitled." I felt
tears fill my eyes. I put my other hand around his neck and
let my fingers cup his chin. But his body was unmovable,
like a rock.

"Turn the car around," my mother said to him, breaking
her long silence. "Don't you know what this place is?" He
looked at her. Their noses were sharp in the moonlight, like
swords.

"We won't stay long." He pulled into a space and shut off
the motor. We were between two cars from whose glued-
together occupants I hid my face. He got out and walked
down to the water's edge and took his rightful eyeful of
moon. He had always told us the best things in life were
free, and tonight he insisted on his fill.

His baggy pants fluttered in the soft wind. He bowed his
head. When he got back into the car, he slammed the door
and drove us home.

That night I considered swallowing all the expired sleeping pills, but I wasn't sure they would do the job. I thought of using the diaphragm, but with who? Instead, I washed my hair with stolen dandruff shampoo and formulated what I would say to Dr. Zucker when I called him the next morning to quit.

Getting a different job turned out not to be a problem. Mr. Wimbush put me in touch with Kirschner Mortgage Company, and they hired me on the spot to post mortgage payments on a huge NCR machine with a thousand buttons. A basket of mail was given to me, and I used a razor-sharp knife to slit the envelopes. The checks went in one pile and the invoices in another. I entered the amount of payment on a square yellow card that I pulled from and then returned to a metal file cabinet. I worked very quickly, in a little cubicle without a window. All down one long row were women in cubicles doing the same thing. Kirschner and his partner worked across the room in separate, elegant, handsomely furnished and carpeted offices.

On my third day there I posted a payment to the account of a man named Frank Stuart. The property was a motel in Hallandale, and twice it had been threatened with foreclosure. I wrote down the name and address of Frank Stuart, taken from his check (he lived in Little River, a suburb of Miami, near the Hialeah Race Track), and I gave it to my father as soon as I got home.

He hugged me so passionately he almost broke my ribs. Then he told my mother what I'd learned and did everything she told him to do, called the police, called the Better Business Bureau, went through the proper channels. My mother, praising him warmly for coming to his senses, helped him by writing all the official letters. It took months. When they finally traced Stuart, they learned he had filed for bankruptcy and left the state. But we were past all that by then. My father had opened a tiny watch-repair shop on

75

Flagler Street, and my mother was now working as an executive secretary for an important lawyer in a big modern office. I was back in school, a senior, and busy sending away for applications to colleges.

One Saturday my mother invited me to her office to fill out the forms there. I was wearing my new aqua cotton shirtwaist dress (my mother had a new black plastic shoulder bag), and we rode the bus together down Collins Avenue, watching the lines of palm trees fanning out along the oceanfront. Walking up Lincoln Road, we both glanced upward at the same instant. Dr. Zucker's window was still boarded up, blank as a blind eye.

In her office, my mother proudly unveiled her electric typewriter for me. I smoothed my skirt and sat down. I turned on the power. Neatly and professionally, my fingers flying like winged angels over the keyboard, I filled out those blessed applications, line by glorious line.

HAIRDOS

On Sunday night the three of us were having a Chicken Snack in Big Boy Bob's when my mother said, quite loudly and unexpectedly, "Oh, where are my babies?" She was staring at the booth behind me, in which a large noisy family sat. They didn't interest me much; my eye was on our waiter, a boy who looked like Timothy Hutton, tall, thin, and sensitive. He was careening around a corner just then, carrying three Big Boy Combinations on his forearm. My mother looked right at me, accusingly. "Where *are* they?" she demanded. "They used to be right here, one clanging her knife and fork together, one under the table looking for her saltine crackers and *you*," she said to me, "*you* were banging your rattle on the high-chair tray." She looked at my father as if he had hidden them from her. They were gone forever, just as I soon would be. One sister was married, and one in college. In the fall I would be on my merry way. I had already applied to Berkeley, Cal State, and, just for kicks, to Harvard. I was ready! My mother couldn't stand the way I sat shaking like a pneumatic drill all the time; during dinner one night I had vibrated the salt shaker right off the edge of the table, smashing it to pieces. My muscles were quivering like a runner's—I was poised, waiting for the gunshot.

My mother's eyes were tired looking. Her hair was half white and half dark brown. She had recently taken me into her confidence about this; she was at a crossroads, she said, and didn't know whether to continue dyeing her hair and avoid the truth for another five or ten years, or to face the facts for good. I don't think I had said the right thing, which was, "What's the difference? You're going to die anyway." "Good point," she'd answered. "I've always known that, but wanted to keep it from you kids in order not to worry you. But now that you know, just remember— when I die—that I had a lot of fun and don't feel too bad or miss me too much."

"Did you?" I asked her. ". . . have fun?" I really wanted an honest answer.

"Yes, of course," she said. "I had a wonderful time. I even had one today, driving to the supermarket. The sun was hanging like an egg yolk over the freeway, and there was one blotch of black smoke coming out of a smokestack, and it was very aesthetic." My mother was worried about the aesthetics of having two tones of hair these days. I had never given the color of her hair much thought. It had always been the same color since the day I was born. I hadn't even known she dyed it till she threw open the question to us one night: "I don't think I want to dye my hair anymore. For one thing, it's deceitful. For another, I hate when those fumes get into my eyes and nose. It can't be good for me. It might even cause cancer. It's ruined two bathrobes already, and—not that you've noticed it—but that's not mold on the bathroom wall. Those little brown spots are Youthful Color, and they won't come off the wall unless I take the paint off too." My father had looked dismayed by the discussion; I supposed it reminded him that he was supposed to paint the bathroom.

"On the other hand, though I don't want to give my daughters the message that staying young is everything, neither do I want them to think that I am leaving the sexual arena entirely."

"*Are* you leaving the sexual arena?" I had asked her. All she and my father talked about was how they were going to manage to pay college tuition for everyone. I wondered if *everyone* ended up talking about money all the time.

The waiter was going by now with two bowls of chili on his forearm. He glanced at me, and then down at my Chicken Snack. He paused, "Everything all right over here?"

"Fine," I said. "But could I please have another little thing of honey? I love my honey sweet," I said, ". . . I mean my chicken sweet," and smiled.

The waiter put down the bowls of chili at the next booth and looked back at me, a little dazed.

"Honey," I reminded him.

He saluted and ran off, tilted at a dangerous angle.

"Where *has* my youth gone?" my mother asked. "Look over there," she added. Across the aisle from us sat an elderly couple, spooning soup into their mouths. The man was frail and had very fine white hair on his head. His wife had hair black as pitch. "Look at her," my mother whispered. "Who does she think she's fooling? Does she think she can pass for thirty-five?"

My father was busily eating his Chicken Snack. We had all ordered Chicken Snacks since that was the special. It came, for some reason, on two pieces of wet, greasy toast. It wasn't bad, really. None of us had gotten anything to drink. We didn't usually in a restaurant because it saved us a lot of money. It was one of the conditions my father had set down about our eating out; soft drinks alone could add three dollars to our bill. We always had water. Sometimes I looked longingly at someone else's icy Coke or triple-thick milkshake while I drank my water, which tasted something like diluted chlorine.

"Now look over there," my mother said. I followed her eyes to where a pair of older women sat, also eating in our section. They both had gray hair, closer to blue-white, set in tight little curls, fresh from a beauty parlor.

"I'm still young," my mother moaned. "Do I want to look like that?"

The waiter came back and dropped six little packets of honey beside my plate.

"I didn't need *this* much," I said, pleased.

79

"No problem," he said. "We have truckloads." His features weren't as fine as Timothy Hutton's, but he had a more relaxed smile. He wore a little leather apron around his hips, with pockets. "Everything fine here?" he asked my parents. "Could I get anyone dessert?"

"I'd like a piece of hot fudge cake with vanilla ice cream," I said, looking at my father. "We could all have some." Sometimes, because we never got anything to drink, he would allow us to get dessert, which we would all share.

"I was thinking," he said, slowly, as if he had given it a lot of thought, ". . . there's that doughnut shop across the street. We could get a whole box of doughnuts for what one dessert costs."

80

"Oh," I said. "But hot fudge cake tastes better than a doughnut, Daddy."

The waiter was standing on one foot, with his pencil poised. He had already laid the bill on the table. He was balanced there, waiting for the signal to pick it up and add on dessert. I loved how tall and thin he was. I loved his shape, his long loose legs, and his smile. I knew my life was going to be rich and full and wonderful, and it would be a lifetime before my hair would be anything but its shining golden brown wavy glorious self.

"Let her have dessert," my mother said to no one in particular. "Life is short."

The baby in the high chair at the next table banged her plastic bottle on the tin top of her tray. "I just don't know where it all went," my mother sighed. I turned around to see where my waiter was; he was behind a mottled glass pane which divided the work area from the eating area. He seemed to be laboring over something. He kept bending down and moving his shoulder, as if he were digging in a hole.

"I guess I believed my girls would be little babies forever. I didn't notice the sixties at all—they just flew by me as if I were buried in the bag of my vacuum cleaner All that news—the war, riots, the music—I didn't pay attention to any of it. I was folding diapers."

"There are still diapers in the trunk of the car," my father said. "I wish you'd get them out."

"I always took care to have extras," my mother said. "I like them there now because they remind me of happy days." She leaned over and wiped a crumb from my father's chin with her napkin.

"I guess I could always use them to clear the fog off the windows," he said.

"I'd rather you didn't," my mother said. "I'd like to keep those diapers for a souvenir."

My waiter was now conferring with two waitresses wearing pert little caps. They, as he had been, were digging in the hole which was not in my line of sight. One would dig, then the other, then my waiter would dig. They seemed quite desperate. I wasn't even very hungry for hot fudge cake now. "Maybe I should go punk," my mother said. "If I dyed my hair green or pink, I wouldn't have this problem to deal with, would I?"

My father looked at my mother as if he were seeing her for the first time in years. "If you're asking me, I don't really like gray hair that much. I liked you better with your old color," he said.

"I liked *you* better with *your* old color," she said, quite passionately, almost furiously. "You liked me better young and I liked *you* better young. But I don't see you dyeing your hair to please *me*."

"Why would I dye my hair?" my father said.

"Why would I dye mine?"

"I don't know," he said, baffled. "I never gave it much thought."

"Don't you think I would like to be young?" my mother said, taking a chunk of ice out of her glass and dropping it in the ashtray where it melted almost instantly.

81

My father looked at his watch. "If we leave in the next five minutes," he said, "we can get home in time to watch *60 Minutes*."

My waiter caught my eye. He looked pained. One of the waitresses had just handed him a silver bullet-shaped urn to hold. He rested his head against its mirrored side and stared at me sadly.

"I used to like sweets," my mother said suddenly. "And then I stopped liking them. Not that I miss them that much, but what makes me sad is that I miss *wanting* them."

"What are they doing back there? Baking the cake?" my father said.

82

"I'll go see," I said, and jumped up, ejecting myself into the aisle. I went behind the mottled glass divider and said to my waiter, "Trouble?"

"Trouble," he said, his face still against the silver urn, his arms around it in a hug.

"Like what?"

"The waitresses from the last shift are supposed to put in a new batch of hot fudge when they go off duty, but they didn't, they never do, and we're trying to get enough together for your cake."

The two waitresses, trying to help my waiter, were leaning over a deep vat, their rumps shaking as they dug for fudge.

"Don't worry about it," I said. I could see myself in the silver side of the urn in his arms, a little distorted, but looking really good. My smile was terrific; my hair was golden. My big wool sweater looked soft, a soft but bright blue color. "Don't take it so seriously," I said. "It's only hot fudge." I smiled at him. He smiled at me.

"I think we've got enough," one of the girls said, from deep in the vat.

"We're going to make it," my waiter said to me, still keeping his eyes right on my face, looking right into my eyes.

"You bet we are," I said. I laughed out loud, and so did

he. I glanced over at my table, where my father was leaning back with his eyes closed, where my mother sat looking at the delicious desserts on the table of the young family, the streak of white in her hair giving her the look of a small frightened wild animal, a skunk or a chipmunk.

"I'll go sit down now," I said, knowing we had to get back into our proper forms.

"I'll bring it," he said with a grin, a signal that we had made contact outside the forms, and that life was fantastic.

I slid into the booth with my parents. In a minute my waiter came to me with a white napkin over his arm and bowed gallantly as he sat the hot fudge cake before me. He put down a clean fork with a sharp clink and grazed my arm as he moved his away.

83

My mouth watered. I had a vision before me of brilliant contrasts: the chocolate cake, the ice cream, the fudge, the whipped cream.

"I wish I wanted some of that," my mother said.

I plunged my fork into it.

"Don't eat it!" she cried. "It's unfair! They have no right to charge us for a mess like that!"

I looked down and saw that the fudge was clotted and clumped around the edges of the plate in irregular brown dots, dropped there, piece by piece, scraped from the far reaches of the emptied vat. The whipped cream had gone a little flat and watery, too. The cake looked dry. But still I wanted to eat it.

My mother was waving now to the waiter. Worried-looking, he came rushing over to us.

"Do you think it's fair for us to have to pay for this mishmosh?"

My father looked embarrassed.

"I think we should at least get a discount," my mother demanded.

The waiter clapped his hands together, thinking. I felt the muscles in my thighs begin to vibrate.

"Would it be okay if I take it off your bill?" the waiter asked nervously, looking over his shoulder.

"But I want it," I said to my mother.

"The fudge is cold. It's got to be cold," she said.

I scooped one of the soft clumps onto my fork and ate it. "It's delicious," I said.

The waiter was crossing it off the bill. He fixed the addition and put the bill down. He hurried away without looking at me.

I continued to eat the hot fudge cake, in big forkfuls, washing it down with my chlorine-scented water. My mother took the fork from her Chicken Snack and wiped it on a napkin. She slid it across the table to my plate and whacked off a corner of fudge cake. "I just want a little taste," she said.

My father looked worried. He said, "You don't understand the principle involved here. If you eat it, you should pay for it, and if you want it taken off the bill, you should have the boy take it away."

"*You* don't understand the principle," my mother said. "It's just a little taste, it's not a crime to want a little taste."

I turned my head and saw the waiter leaning against the mottled glass divider, one hand inserted between two buttons of his brown Big Boy vest. He was watching me. Rather, he was admiring me—he smiled to make it clear. My heart swelled.

"Here, Mom," I said, sliding my entire plate her way. "I'm stuffed. You have all the rest."

"Well—I don't know. But okay, only if Daddy will share it with me."

My father opened his mouth to protest, but my mother was already holding the fork to his lips. She pushed some loose chocolate crumbs toward his mouth with her other hand, which she held cupped under his chin. She fed him like a baby and in spite of himself my father laughed—he actually laughed—and gobbled up the sweets.

84

A VIEW OF
BOSTON COMMONS

Lalia's office window looked directly upon Boston Commons and across to the great gold dome of the State House. (When she wrote her mother about this vista, her mother, who lived in Florida, sent her back an old *Saturday Evening Post* cover which boasted Lalia's very view. "You are a lucky girl," her mother wrote. "A very lucky girl.")

Lalia supposed she was lucky; she hoped so. She was newly married (six months)—and she had been engaged before college graduation, an essential requirement of being lucky in the late fifties. She had even had a year of graduate school in English on a fellowship at Brandeis before she took her present job as "editorial assistant" at Parker Publishing House. That too was luck: for an English major to get a job in publishing. Of course, she would have preferred to stay on in school, like her husband. But all her girlfriends were supporting their husbands through their PhDs—she had agreed to it because it was part of the master plan. Her pay was fifty-five dollars a week. Her boss, Mr. Cromie, a pink-faced, white-haired former professor, now an editor of history texts, apologized that the company had only this office to give her—on the fifth floor—while all the other education-department offices were on the sixth. But he promised he would frequently be down to see her. She'd have plenty of work, there was no reason to worry they'd forget about her.

Each morning, as this morning, she kissed Bill goodbye,

trying to picture—without rancor—his day: a leisurely rising (after the heat had finally come on and warmed their
attic apartment), English muffins and jam and coffee while
he read about early liturgical music, and—if it weren't
snowing or raining too hard—a brisk walk down Mass. Ave.
to Widener Library. Later he would attend his one class of
the day, a graduate seminar taught by a famous scholar.

She left him under the electric blanket, pulled on her
boots and coat, and went to wait for the trolley, shivering on
the corner of Prentiss Street, standing in slush, and then—
at the Harvard Square station—squeezed herself into the
train to Boston. She was unable to read on the train;
instead she studied the faces of the travelers and looked at
her own distorted reflection in the curve of her gold wedding band. She was surely lucky; she and Bill were doing all
the things in the right order. The formula promised suc-
cess: moderation, patience, practicality, self-control. Two
months before their wedding, at spring break (she was in a
dorm at Brandeis then, he in a room in Waltham), they had
taken a trip to Plymouth Rock and had faced the choice of
driving back before nightfall or taking a hotel room. No one
knew where they were; no one would miss them. She remembered standing with Bill beside Plymouth Rock in her
new orange canvas shoes that matched her cotton skirt. The
two of them were weighing the alternatives. Bill's eyes were
somewhere far out in the ocean as they deliberated. She
weighed her alternatives and decided she wanted to spend
the night with him. His scale balanced another way: "We've
waited this long, Lalia. Why not wait a little longer?"

They'd waited. They'd done everything to order so far.
They were doing it now.

She stared at her wedding ring and at the heavy shoes of
the passengers on the train. Boots, galoshes, clear plastic
slip-overs, feet ready to move, shuffle, hurry, run to work.
She thought of the library—any library—the shelves and
shelves of books; the long wooden tables, the warm squares

of sunshine coming in the great windows (or the comforting blasts of heat on snowy days), the freedom to think your own thoughts, the time to study. She had loved studying, been good at it. Maybe better than Bill. But Bill was going to be a professor; she was not. Was it The Great Man at the University who had prevented this? Or other forces? She recalled the meanness in his face that day she had come to his office. He was typing. He wrote books. He refused to stop typing; words spewed out of him. He typed as she or other students talked to him, he was famous for it. She made her request. His gray hair was thin on his round head. The rims of his wire glasses pressed into his temples. **87** He was an ambitious man; she had known of his reputation long before she had come here—and now he was her advisor, as well as head of the department. He was in control of her future.

He talked to her as he typed, not once looking at her face. "Let's face it, Lalia; you're as smart as any student here, your grades are as good. You say you want me to recommend you for the PhD fellowship. But there are men in the English department here who need those fellowships. You're only a girl, Lalia, you have other options. No, I'm not going to recommend you for going on. If you pass your orals, you'll get a terminal MA. And if you don't pass your orals, which as you know is a distinct possibility, you're plain terminal, my dear. That's just the way it has to be." She waited for more, but there was only the ding of his carriage-return bell.

On her way back to her dorm in the snow, she decided she would simply not take her orals. She believed he would never pass her, and she would not allow him to humiliate her further. Struggling up the hill to her room, she took a flying fall on a patch of ice. Her legs flailed in the air as if she were a cockroach turned on its back. When she regained her balance, she turned over on her hands and knees and crawled toward the square dull building called

Schwartz Hall, where she lived, next to the turreted and
elegant dorm called The Castle. She had been fated to
Schwartz, others to The Castle. As simple and as critical a
matter as being born boy or girl.

Across the aisle of the subway train the flash of a white
cane caught Lalia's eye. She recognized the same couple she
always saw—the woman in her green coat with the fur
collar, her hair rolled under in a style from the thirties, and
the man beside her in his black topcoat, his plaid muffler
carefully tucked into his collar. In her lap the woman held
the two brown paper bags, as she always did, their tops
folded down neatly.

The train rumbled through the blackness. Lalia never
made her own lunch in the morning. She found it hard
enough to shiver into her clothes in the freezing attic, race
for the trolley, get to work on time. At lunchtime she
wandered the streets, looked in store windows, ate a sandwich at Woolworth's counter. She had a secret vice: once a
month she took her own photo in a curtained booth at
Woolworth's. Each time, for her twenty-five cents, she got
four black-and-white pictures of herself on a strip. She was
letting her hair grow, and, as each month passed, she
seemed to be turning into a new woman. Perhaps by the end
of the year she would be completely transformed. She was
waiting to see if it happened.

The train pulled into Park Street station. The woman in
the green coat stood up and helped the man stand; she
thrust one of the paper bags into his hand. He held the
white cane in his other. She kissed him firmly on the lips.
She kissed him twice, as always. His eyes seemed to burn
phosphorescent in their whiteness. Then the woman pushed
him straight out the door. Lalia stepped out right behind
him.

The woman hurried back to her seat; she stared out the
window at the man till the train doors closed and the train
pulled away. This moment, when the woman was being

88

parted from her lover (for surely lovers they were), this
moment always brought tears to Lalia's eyes. How close she
must be to the edge, that she almost could not bear it. She
wondered if she would ever love her own husband that way.
The man stood, his head cocked, taking stock of his state of
aloneness. Then he began to walk, very slowly, toward the
stairs, then slowly up them, clicking the cane from side to
side while Lalia followed behind him, her arms out as if to
catch him should be fall backwards. Once in the air, outside, with the sky above, the pigeons whirling by, she went
her own way (she had to) and he went his. Sometimes, just
after she left him, Lalia actually let out a few wild sobs as   **89**
she thought of the woman going on alone in the train, not
knowing where he was and what might befall him.

On her desk was the usual: an article in manuscript for
inclusion in the anthology she was editing; a notice from
Mr. Cromie to be sure to get the wording of the permissions
correct. A New York publisher was threatening to sue about
a work of Camus which didn't get proper credit.

On her windowsill pigeons crowded against the glass, one
landing atop the other, awaiting her service. She daily
brought cracker crumbs in a plastic bag for them. She had
to use all her strength to open the window, but she could
now do it. (In the beginning she had to ask Harry, the
elevator man, to help her.)

Today the sun glinted off the dome of the State House; the
world was far away and far below; she felt like Rapunzel
about to let down her hair. But she had to grow it much
longer first.

From down the hall she heard the clack of typewriters;
the chatter of the secretaries from the art department.
They wore new outfits to work as often as they could afford
to; when she listened to their exchanges she heard mostly
gasps of admiration. "Where *did* you get that dress? How
much did you pay for it? Don't tell me!"

Lalia couldn't do it. She simply couldn't join them. In

any case, they ignored her because she wore high socks to work, socks with penny-loafers, and boots, too, while they wore stockings and stiletto-type high heels. One day Mr. Cromie called her into his office: "I've heard some unkind things about you, Lalia, that you do not dress in a way that pleases the other secretaries."

"I'm not a secretary, Mr. Cromie," she said. "And it's really fortunate, isn't it, that you and the other men who work here can wear socks and trousers on a day like this, when it's six degrees outside." His gaze became confused. "Don't worry," she said. "I'm on the fifth floor; I don't walk around in your department too much, I shouldn't be too big an embarrassment to you."

"You could talk to Martha Gratz," he said. "She might be able to suggest a compromise. Somewhat lower heels than the others wear, perhaps."

Martha Gratz was Mr. Cromie's assistant. She had worked for Parker's for thirty years; she came before Mr. Cromie and would be here after him. She knew Mr. Cromie's work better than he did, but she was still an assistant. Only men were editors at Parker. Martha wore gray suits and black shoes. She shaved her chin. Lalia feared that if she stayed on here, in thirty years she'd be in Martha Gratz's seat.

But she wouldn't stay on. She was destined to have babies. Soon. When Bill got his degree and a job. That was all part of the master plan.

Lalia fed cracker crumbs to the pigeons and envied them their wings. They flew away to the top of the golden dome; they swooped and dipped and soared. Lalia was fastened to her wooden desk chair: she had to check for misplaced commas and quotation marks. She had to make the professors who wrote the articles look as smart as they were supposed to be.

By lunchtime she had finished her work for the day. This often happened, that she finished her work before the workday was over. Because she was quick and efficient, she had to pretend that she was working from one to five o'clock. What was there to do? Yet it was unthinkable to go home, forbidden. Mr. Cromie was not likely to bring down new work; if he came to her office at all, it was in the morning. If she should go upstairs to ask him what to do next, he would become embarrassed—he never had any work waiting for her. He sometimes asked Martha Gratz if she had anything for Lalia to do, but Martha Gratz was so efficient she had nearly nothing to do herself.

Lalia again opened the window and a chill wind blew in. She imagined her husband in the Harvard library; she imagined his life later on, after they had children, during which he would continue to go to libraries, and she would be at home. Her mother had been at home all her life; her mother had gotten very good at doing crossword puzzles. Her mother was a whiz with words; she knew more words than the dictionary contained. In fact, she was a Scrabble champion; she had won a title in a local competition in Miami Beach. Her mother would have loved libraries, big ones, had she ever gotten near any.

Lalia put on her boots and heavy coat and her scarf and went down in the elevator. Christmas was coming—the Salvation Army was out, the kneeless, toeless, thighless beggars were out; little tinseled reindeer were prancing in the windows of Filene's Department Store. In Woolworth's she ordered her regular: a bacon, tomato, and lettuce club sandwich with potato chips. When she finished it, she ordered a malted as well and spun on her stool as she drank it, watching the shoppers.

She was staring idly toward the street when she saw the Great Man from the English Department come into Woolworth's with a beautiful blonde on his arm. She was most certainly not the Great Man's wife. Everyone at school knew his wife—she was overweight, and she was famous for wearing plaid slacks.

The Great Man parted the curtain of the photo booth and

stepped inside with the blonde. Lalia heard their laughter.
The green curtain was short; she could see their four legs
being arranged and rearranged in the small space. Soon
one set of legs (the legs in stockings) hung over the other set,
the ones in trousers. The muted flash of the photo light sent
a thrilling jolt into Lalia's head. She took the silver canister
of her malted, along with a straw, and went to wait her turn
outside the booth. After the fourth flash, the occupants of
the booth did not immediately come out. Information written inside and outside the booth said that there was a two-
minute waiting period while the machine ground and
drilled and shook the pictures into being.

92

Lalia waited patiently. She had no work on her desk in
the office. There was no reason to leave this spot. She
waited, holding the icy silver container. When the strip of
pictures came sliding down the chute, she was there to catch
it. In the first frame the Great Man was kissing the blonde.
In the second, the Great Man was sticking out his tongue
quite foolishly while the blonde bit his ear. She hadn't yet
absorbed the images on the third and fourth frames when
the Great Man emerged through the curtain, balding head
first. He peered, puzzled, at Lalia through his wire-rimmed
glasses.

"Hello, Professor," she said. "It's nice to see you again."

He appeared unable to think of a word to say, this man
who never stopped throwing out words. He could hardly
turn away from her to his typewriter just now.

Lalia took her time, stopping to draw a sip from her
straw with a strident, sucking sound. "I have a job now,"
she said. "I'm no longer in school, you know."

He nodded, staring at the strip of pictures in her hand.
"That's too bad," he said. "You were a fine student."

"Do you really think so?"

"Oh yes," he said. "Without a doubt."

"That was a hard reading list you gave us," she said. "All
the Shakespeare plays. All of Pope and Swift. Chaucer.

Byron. The Restoration comedies. I never took the oral exam, you know. I had a feeling I would never pass."

"It's a pity," he said. His face was red.

"I think so, too," Lalia said. She looked at the blonde and finished her thought. "But you know how it is, these things hardly matter—for us girls."

She handed the pictures over to him; he took the strip as if he might take the tail of a dead rat. "It was interesting bumping into you," Lalia said.

"Yes," he said, "I can see that."

"I've got to get back to work now."

He smiled, a sickly, nauseated smile.

"Bye-bye," Lalia said to the blonde.

When she left them, she walked toward Boston Commons. She found a bench with a good view of her office window and sat herself down among the pigeons. The air was cold and crisp. The dome of the State House seemed to float toward her and become a golden crown upon her head.

Now and then during the afternoon, she glanced up toward the room where she was supposed to be sitting at her desk, arranging commas.

93

RESCUE

The night was cold. Janet, her arm linked in Danny's, leaned on the rail of the observation platform which overlooked the churning rainbow of motion below in the float-building arena. High above them, floodlights burned in the domed roof of the steel shed. Janet peered into the brilliant circle of lights and flowers, seeking the form of her younger nephew, eleven-year-old David. She found him sitting on a high scaffold almost level with her eyes, a red-and-white "Tournament of Roses" pin on his blue jacket, his thin legs in blue jeans, his large feet hanging down, swinging slightly. She was greatly impressed by his ability to work so steadfastly in these inhospitable circumstances. The tip of his tongue quivered in concentration as he dipped the calyx of each pink rose into the glue pot, and gently, patiently screwed the hardening blossom into the forehead of the injured boy on the litter. The smell of chemicals—paint, adhesive, turpentine—was overwhelming.

Janet shivered and pulled tighter the belt of her new goosedown coat. Wine-colored, cloud-soft, it comforted her. She had bought it less than a week ago, on sale the day after Christmas, and modeled it proudly for Danny when she got home.

"It's truly a fine coat," he had said, ". . . but maybe more for the Swiss Alps than for Southern California."

"It protects me," she had answered in defense. "I feel armored in it."

"Against what?" he had asked.

"Nothing specific," she had answered. "Just . . . everything." Now she rubbed herself further into the coat's feathery depths and searched for her older nephew, Abram, whom she had seen a few moments earlier sweeping the cement floor—pushing, with a wide black broom, piles of crushed petals and broken stems into a small mountain.

Hawkers below were selling red plastic roses. A six-foot-high wooden thermometer stood beside the coffee concession announcing how far the city had come toward its goal for contributions to the float-building fund.

96 "You know, I can't see Abram anywhere," Janet said quietly to Danny, her heart jumping a bit. Her constant nightmare was that she would someday—again—have to be the carrier of bad news to her sister, Carol. A little over two years ago she had had to bring Carol news of her husband's suicide.

She looked in the crowd of visitors milling around the float for a boy almost a foot taller than he had been on the day when he and his mother and brother had moved to the house across the street from Janet—for what small care and comfort she could offer them. Recently she had been urging Carol to try to let the boys out of her sight a little more often, to give them some slack. She had assured her sister that allowing them to work on the Rose float over the Christmas holiday was bound to be good for them. The park where the float was built was only a half-block from their house. There would be lots of adults supervising the soldering, the painting, the glueing. The neighborhood was benign, reasonably safe. Why not let them go?

But now that she could not see Abram she was beginning to feel frightened herself. The city was full of strangers and tourists on this last day of the year.

"He'll turn up in a second," Danny said, poking her shoulder through the thick coat. She sensed he was about to make a joke—she even knew what it would be. "Don't worry," he said, proving to her how well she read him, "we can always call out the search-and-rescue team."

"Very funny," she said, making a wry face at him. What a grand irony it would be if Abram disappeared here, where nearly all the members of their city's famous search-and-rescue mountain-climbing team were having coffee below, near the wooden thermometer. In fact, the float, coming to life in front of them at this moment, was a demonstration of their fortitude and courage—a re-creation of the rescue of a child about to be saved by the team. Two mammoth bloodhounds dominated the design, their great heavy heads bobbing, their tongues, made of bark and seed, lolling realistically. The dogs' fur, thickly ruffled pelts of bronze mums, shone magnificently in the floodlights which were aimed downward from metal struts in the dome of the enclosure.

"They'll never be able to move it out of here by ten," Danny said. "It's nine-thirty now. They'll be lucky if they get down to the starting arena before midnight. Look—they haven't even begun on the cockpit of the chopper yet."

The float's papier-mâché helicopter, covered with marigold petals and cornhusks, its blades ablaze with red and yellow carnations, hovered (supported, David had told Janet earlier, by cables covered with fire grass from Hawaii) over the scene, about to effect the rescue of the little boy stranded on a mountain ledge. Beneath the rocky outcropping, where the child lay unconscious on a litter, the gleaming eyes of deer, raccoons, and a bighorn sheep peered out from a forest of moss and pampas grass.

"Oh, thank God, there he is," Janet sighed. Abram, lanky and serious-looking, had just come in a rear door, carrying in the cradle of his arms a great spray of lilies, apparently brought from the refrigerated truck parked outside. He climbed onto the float where he hurried toward a young woman dressed in a white Tournament of Roses official jumpsuit. She looked powerful and efficient, with her gold hair shining in the light, a reflective glow emanating from her white suit. Abram transferred the lilies to her with extreme care and tenderness, as if he were placing a baby in its mother's arms. He and the girl talked for a moment, she whispering in his ear, and he responding with a nod of his head. Briefly, the girl swung her face up, and Janet saw that it was Lucie Franklin, their neighbors' eighteen-year-old daughter. She looked quite different tonight, redefined somehow by the authority conferred upon her by the official uniform.

98

High above Abram, on the scaffold, his brother David was gently, almost passionately, stroking the organic eyelashes of the motionless flower child, as if the two of them were quite alone, deep in the forest. David's face expressed so much concern, so much sadness, that Janet thought he might believe at this moment that the child's plight was real. But just then, Abram glanced up and saw his brother's feet hanging above him.

"Hey, Dave," he called up. "You want to see the real bloodhounds? Lucie says Coach Puller is bringing them in right now. Come on down. We can pet them if we like."

"Sure," David called, casting an apologetic glance at the boy who lay helpless, his head to the side, his mouth slightly open, a single tear made of hardened sap on his pale cheek. David began to descend from the scaffold.

"Who's Coach Puller?" Danny asked.

"That's him, right there," Janet explained, pointing, as a large, bearded, genial-looking man walked in the rear door, preceded by two large, genial-looking bloodhounds. "He's a very big hero around here. He's the captain of the search-and-rescue team, he drives the city ambulance, and he coaches the boys' Little League."

"Well, I guess I couldn't be expected to know all *that*," Danny said. "We have *daughters*."

● ● ●

Their daughters were away this New Year's Eve, sleeping along the parade route with their friends. Tonight David and Abram were going to carry on the family tradition of making chocolate chip cookies at the stroke of midnight. While the boys were still working on the float, Janet set out the makings—flour and eggs, vanilla and brown sugar and chocolate chips, while Carol sat at the table, her thin face reflected in the stainless steel mixing bowl.

"We *could* let them make the mess at my house," she said without enthusiasm.

"You'll have enough commotion over there tomorrow, when the relatives come," Janet assured her.

"I can't imagine that Mom and Aunt Gert will actually come, not after their moaning about the Rose Bowl traffic and the dangerous drunk drivers all over the place . . ."

"By now you should know their style, Carol. First they have to complain forever, and then, when they finally come, they can assure each other what a big mistake they made."

"You really sound like you're looking forward to company," Carol said.

"Actually, I'm not," Janet admitted. "I don't know why—it's just that I want to start the new year feeling up, and I have the feeling they want to start it down. It's in their genes. I just hope eventually I can cancel it out of mine. According to them, we live on the verge of catastrophe, and the natural state of life should reasonably be terror. When life is going smoothly (by some unlikely oversight), we must always remember that it's certain to get terrible soon."

"Well, isn't that the truth?" Carol asked in a flat, odd voice. She flipped back the kitchen curtain. "I think it's time to go down to the park. I see flashing lights—the police escort. The float is probably getting ready to leave."

"Let's go then," Janet said, wiping her hands on a dish-towel. "Danny?" she called down the hall. "Want to walk down to the park again? We think it's time."

"Sure—" he called, coming into the kitchen, lifting

Janet's coat off a chair and holding it out to her. "Time to
re-enter the Arctic Circle."

Outside they met their next-door neighbors—Mary and
John Franklin—just coming down their driveway.

"Happy New Year, folks!" John greeted them. He was a
stocky man, gray-haired, about fifty. "Did you know our
Lucie is driving the float tonight?"

"No, I didn't!" Janet said. "I just saw her down at the
park in her official white uniform a little while ago, but I
never made the connection. That's great that she's driving
100 this year. I know how hard she's worked on the float—every
year since about fourth grade!"

"Yup," John said proudly. "They promised her—she
could do it as soon as she turned eighteen. Her life's ambi-
tion. But, the poor kid, she has to be awake all night."

"The young are strong," his wife said. "They can take it,
John. Don't worry about her. It's the biggest night of her
life."

As they walked the half-block to the park, they saw, in
the moonlight, the gleaming outlines of the float as it lumbered, like a monolith, down the dirt road, over the sand-
smoothed curb and turned very slowly onto the main street.
Runners ran ahead with long Y-shaped poles, holding up
electric wires so that the top of the float would not snag
them. A small crowd lined the street, cheering and ap-
plauding as the great bloodhounds shimmered above them
like prehistoric monsters blocking out the moon. The float
rumbled past, heavy as a tank. Janet felt the vibrations
from it flow through the center of her heart.

David and Abram were running beside it, gathering a few
loose flowers which fell to the street. David yelled, "Right
on, Lucie! Bring home the Governor's Trophy!" The perfume left in the float's wake was palpable, cloyingly sweet.

"Poor Lucie. She's hidden underneath ten tons of
flowers," John said. "She can't see a thing in there. All she
can do is look through a hole at her feet and follow the blue

line. A navigator has to guide her from up above, tell her
how fast to go, when to stop and start. A pity, isn't it, that
she'll miss the whole parade. Well, I guess she can see the
replay on television tomorrow afternoon."

"John!" Mary said. "You forgot to bring the drinks for
her!"

"Oh, hell's bells," he said. "I'll be right back!" He made
a U-turn and began running up the street toward his house.

"She's got to have something to drink under there, it gets
very hot," Mary explained. "We had the cooler all packed
and ready to go and John just forgot it in the excitement."

Carol was calling to her sons: "Stand back. Don't get so
close. Be careful. You'll get your feet run over." The boys
were dancing alongside the float, patting it goodbye. As the
float passed beneath a street light, the yellow argon beams
illuminated the deathly still boy on the litter.

101

"I made his face, Mom," David yelled. "The whole
thing."

"Very good," Carol called back. She looked distracted,
not really there with them. Janet remembered all the other
years they had stood here, watching the float leave, when
Carol's husband had stood with them at the curb.

There was an irregular clanking sound in the dark street
behind them, and John emerged from the darkness, grip-
ping a heavy cooler in his two hands. It bounced against his
belly as he ran. "I put two more six-packs of Coke in here,"
he gasped, "just in case Lucie needs them." The cans were
banging against one another. He was panting, racing after
the float, which was now rolling a little faster along the
road.

"Take it easy," his wife called after him.

"Yeah, I know—" he managed to say. "I'm really too old
for this."

After the float had gone on its way, the boys came back to
Janet's house to work on the chocolate chip cookies. The
color was high on their cheeks. Abram stirred the batter

with powerful circles of his arm while David measured out
the brown sugar. Danny paced the length of the kitchen,
yawning.

"Do you think you can stick it out?" Janet asked him.
"Only ten minutes to midnight."

"I don't know if I can stay awake that long," Danny said.
"It gets harder every year."

"I could easily stay up all night," Abram said proudly.
"Next year I'm going to sleep on the parade route."

"We'll see," his mother said.

"I'll be almost fourteen. You'll have to let me."

102   "We'll talk about it then."

"Here, have some batter." David offered his mother a
fingertip full of dough. "It's great raw."

"No thanks," Carol said. "I'm not into thrills like that
anymore."

A flashing light lunged across the window glass, startling
them. The scream of a siren began and in the same instant
was cut short. It started up again only to blip off suddenly.
Danny switched off the kitchen lights. They stood in the
dark, frozen still, staring out at the red flashing eye of
whatever was beyond the black windowpane. Like a lighthouse beam, it spun around, blanking out the blinking red
and green bulbs of Christmas ornaments hanging under the
eaves of the houses on the street.

"It's the paramedics!" Abram cried, his voice cracking.

"They've stopped right next-door, Janet," Danny said.
Her husband spoke in a tone which wrenched her gut. The
boys were already out the door and on the front walk.

"Take your jackets," Carol admonished them, but she
followed them outside wearing only her thin shirt herself.

"They're at the Franklins," Janet gasped. "Oh my God.
Do you think . . .?"

Police cars came tearing up the street. The fire chief
pulled up and jumped from his red truck. A pandemonium
of flashing lights tore open the sky.

"Keep back, keep back," a police officer commanded.

"Coach Puller!" Abram called out as his coach ran with his medical box from the ambulance into the Franklins' house. Carol smacked him suddenly, on the shoulder, very hard. "Don't distract him, idiot!" she said. Janet saw that Carol was shivering, that tears were running down her cheeks. She went to her, put her arms around her.

"Not again," Carol sobbed. She was shaking uncontrollably. "Not that nice man, not now, not tonight, not ever, not when their daughter is driving the float."

Janet felt the chill spread from her sister to herself. They were both turning to ice, standing there. Just as two firemen carried John Franklin out on the litter, firecrackers burst into stars up and down the street. Horns and hoots and gunshots turned the year over. Janet heard, louder than any other sound, the flap-flap of the heart pump fastened to her neighbor's chest.

"Easy," Coach Puller said, every line of his body leaning toward the man's mouth as he gave him air from his own lungs. "Shut the pump and lift up—*fast!*" There was a tiny silence while horns raged and whistles shrieked in the air about them. Coach Puller leaped into the ambulance with John Franklin; Mary Franklin was helped in, the doors were closed after her, and someone jumped behind the wheel of the ambulance and roared away. Janet was left with the picture of Mary Franklin imprinted upon her mind: her terrified face, her purse on her arm, a thin sweater over her shoulders, her body being pushed up into the ambulance.

"He won't make it," one of the policemen said to a neighbor's inquiry. "They couldn't get him started again. Hell of a time to have this happen. Someone has to go and tell his daughter. Someone has to find her and bring her home."

In the morning, Janet was sick. She lay in bed, watching the parade on television without sound, watching the bands and the silver-saddled horses go by, the marching girls in

103

their fringed boots, the drum majorettes, fearless in their shorts and sparkling tunics. She was consumed with nausea and stomach cramps. From time to time, she staggered to the bathroom and vomited. She wouldn't speak. Danny brought her icy apple juice and she nodded thanks, not meeting his eyes. She was afraid that when he left the room he might have a heart attack in the hall. She would never see him again. Her happy life would be over. Was it true that this vision was locked in her genes: the conviction that in life we are always on the verge of catastrophe—that even when things are going well we must remember that they're certain to turn bad momentarily?

104

The family visit was called off. Carol phoned and spoke to Danny, who answered the bedside phone. She told him the relatives didn't want to come and catch Janet's germ. She also told Danny to relay a message to Janet: that the boys had learned from a friend that Mr. Franklin had died, but that his daughter was driving the float in the parade anyway. "Lucie decided to do it," Danny relayed the message to Janet, "because she said her father would have wanted her to."

Janet did not even open her eyes as he spoke.

"Carol says she wants to speak to you," Danny said, holding out the phone to her. Weakly, Janet reached up and took the receiver from him.

"Remember," Carol said, "She's hanging in there, that's the important thing."

"Okay—if you say so," Janet whispered. She handed the phone back to Danny and stumbled out of bed and into the bathroom. When she came back, shivering, she crawled under her covers.

"Do you want anything?" Danny asked her. "Can I get you anything?"

"Bring me my down coat," she said.

He brought it and laid it gently over her quilt.

"Thank you." She covered her face with its cool nylon fabric and kneaded the feathers in a soft agony.

"Here comes our float," Danny said gently, patting her knee as he sat on the edge of the bed. Janet uncovered her face.

On the screen the bloodhounds came into view, their hinged jaws slack and slavering. The red and yellow helicopter blades rotated against a blank sky. The eyes of the little boy on the litter were still closed, the permanent tear cemented to his cheek. Supporting the weight of ten thousand roses and lilies was Lucie Franklin, bravely sitting in the dark, staring through the hole, steering along the blue line, counting on the goodness of others to help her through.

105

II

THE ANNA STORIES: A NOVELLA

"RAD, MAN"

On the TV screen some thug with long blond hair named Hulk Hogan was wrestling some other hooligan wearing leopard-skin jockey shorts. Their grunts, as they hit the floor, sounded to Anna like a hippopotamus in labor.

Anna's grandsons, Abram and David, leaned forward on the couch, staring at the screen without blinking—two complete morons. At each sound of a human head hitting the canvas, a burst of unintelligible speech came out of Abram's mouth and his bare, tanned knees came up as if he were having a fit. (Despite the fact that it was December, he was wearing some garish flowered shorts that had cost Carol thirty dollars.) He leaned over suddenly and punched his brother who cried out, "Rad, man! Rad!" Then the two boys proceeded to punch each other violently for about twenty seconds.

Carol was calmly reading the paper and drinking her coffee at the table. Either she was deaf, or dead, to ignore the carnage taking place here. How could her daughter, how could *anyone*, live like this? These boys weren't civilized human beings. They were cave men just out of the bush. The sounds that came forth from these children's mouths were unbelievable (and not only from their mouths). Anna felt sorry for Carol, but what could she do? She was supposed to mind her own business no matter how bad things got around here.

She scrutinized her older grandson. He was just fifteen

and was six feet three inches tall. His good looks were no fault of his. Plus he was adopted, and God only knew what else would turn up in him. He held in his lap a soup bowl piled with eight scoops of Heavenly Hash ice cream and raised to dangerous heights with swirls of fake whipped cream shot from a can. Anna had noticed that he'd emptied into his dish the entire ice cream carton and the entire can of whipped cream which her daughter had just bought yesterday at the supermarket. He'd only stopped his frantic squirting from the nozzle when the last blurps had spat dots of cream all over himself and the couch. And this was right after he'd eaten a gigantic dinner—three burritos with red sauce (whatever was in them Anna should never know from it). The food in this house didn't last twenty-four hours after Carol dragged in two hundred dollars' worth from the car, bag after heavy bag. And did the boys help her carry in the groceries? No, they were too busy watching TV. "Later! I'll do it *later!*" was their refrain—a reflex wailed constantly, whether or not anyone was asking them to do anything. ("Goodnight," Anna would say, and they'd yell, "I'll do it later!")

Anna had addressed them many times (both in and out of their mother's presence) in the two weeks she'd been recuperating here. She had told them, speaking very slowly, in a way that even a total retard could understand, that they only had one mother in this life and she was the only one they were ever going to get and they had better treat her with respect. She wasn't going to last forever and at the rate they were wearing her out she wasn't even going to last another week. *Especially* with no father around to keep them in line. By the way their eyes went blank, Anna knew she should have saved her energy. It all went in one ear and right out the other. As for Carol, if she were listening to Anna give her speech, her eyes got small and hard in a way that made Anna's heart skip a few beats. But she wasn't going to be intimidated. She had her piece to say and she was going to say it; maybe it wouldn't sink in till ten years from now, and maybe never, but at least she could feel she'd done her part.

Now Abram stopped gobbling ice cream long enough to pull off his shoes and socks and toss them at Mr. T, the dog. Between the smells that came from both ends of the animal, and those that came from Abram's feet, it was no wonder Anna couldn't eat here, was nauseated all the time. The instant she got better from her fall, she would be out of here and back to her own apartment like a shot. In fact, as soon as she got home to LA, she planned to start a lawsuit against the high school where she went to her night classes—whose pothole she had fallen in and thereby broken her foot. She couldn't *wait* to get home. God save her from the day she would ever have to live with either of her two children—this arrangement was no good and what's more it could only get worse.

"Time to light the Chanukah candles," Carol announced from the table. "Also time to rewind the movie, boys, because we have to return the tape to Leo's before nine."

"This is a *rented* movie?" Anna asked her daughter. "I thought this was just regular TV junk."

"It's only ninety-nine cents to rent a movie on a weeknight, Mom," Carol said. "It's no big deal."

"Why is it that everything they do has to cost money? Didn't they ever hear of reading a book?"

"They can't learn everything from books," Carol said. "They get plenty of that in school."

"They can learn something from baseball cards?"

"Yeah," Abram interrupted, "especially from baseball cards. Hey, Mom—I need money for another pack. You promised. Brian got Peewee Reese, the lucky dog."

"I know exactly what they learn from TV," Anna said. "They learn how to murder drug pushers and how to throw someone out a window. But what talents do they get from baseball cards?"

111

"Well, for one thing," Carol said, "they trade and sell them. They learn about the realities of the market place."

"Reality! This is reality? VCRs, video games, new bicycles, new skateboards—they think it all comes to them at the snap of a finger."

"My children know more about reality, Mom," Carol said coldly, "than anyone their age should ever know." Anna knew exactly to what Carol was referring; her daughter was going to use that as an excuse to spoil her sons for the rest of their lives.

"Rad!" breathed Abram toward the TV screen. The gorilla in the jockey shorts was now spinning the blond guy over his head like a helicopter's blades. Anna closed her eyes till the thump occurred and only opened them when she was sure the body had hit down. Abram swung his long arm forward and hit a button on the VCR. The screen began to flutter and show the wrestlers doing everything backwards. They rose up from the floor like ballerinas.

In actual fact Anna was not against Carol's spending money on the boys for cultural purposes—music lessons would have been fine, even *English* lessons! But Hebrew lessons? That was going too far. The way the kids fought Carol, who literally had to force them into the car twice a week to go to *shul*, was a disgrace. Why was she wasting her time? Did she think these hoodlums of hers were going to turn into little rabbis? Again, on this issue, Anna had plenty to say, but maybe this wasn't the right moment.

"Now let's do the candles," Carol said firmly. "Then we'll go to Leo's."

"I don't want to go," David said. "I'm busy."

"I'll only go if you take me to Big Five first," Abram said. "I need new tennis shoes."

"Not tonight," Carol said. "You just got new tennis shoes."

"I didn't *just* get them. Besides, Mr. T chewed holes in them."

"That's because you throw him your shoes as if they're meat bones," Carol said. "Now—whose turn is it to light the candles?"

"His," both boys said, each pointing at his brother.

"All right, you do it tonight, David. I think Abram did it last night." Carol went to get the matches from a high shelf. As she reached for them, Anna saw how thin her arm was, how lank and frail she seemed. To handle boys like this, a person would need to have the strength of an ox. To do it all without a man to help—that was the real tragedy.

On the counter between the kitchen and the family room sat the menorah which had belonged to Anna's mother. It was made of tin. Her mother had paid five cents for it in 1910 in a grocery store in Brooklyn. Anna, having long since had enough of Jewish nonsense herself, had asked her daughters a few years ago which one wanted the family heirloom. She didn't have the heart to throw it out. It was so lightweight Carol had had to steady it on the counter with the end of one of Abram's small barbells. The tin was embossed with the image of a real menorah: brass—heavy and authentic. The tin cylinders which held the swirled, colored candles were deformed, pressed out of shape by time. Each night that the boys had been forced by their mother to light the candles, Anna had felt something close in her throat, some soundless gasp escape her. Her own Abram had been observant; he had lit the candles seriously, said the prayer. To whom? For what? What had his prayers got him but leukemia at fifty-five? And left her here, lost in this life without him, an intruder in her daughter's household, an extra person who belonged to no one.

"Where's the box of candles?" David demanded. He had a voice like a hog-caller. Words didn't exit his lips, they exploded forth. "I don't want two yellows next to each other. They look gross. Who put them in like that?"

"I did," Carol said.

"What are you, some kind of retard?" David accused her.

113

"Don't speak to your mother that way," Anna said.

"But she is," Abram defended his brother. "Mom's just out of it all the time. She's a total nerd."

This boy who was now addressing Anna and insulting his mother was the child who bore Anna's husband's name and *wasn't even from their genuine family.* She didn't believe in adoption and now she had doubts about personal childbirth as well. Even her other daughter's children—college girls now—were not always to her taste, to say the least. Their genes, of course, were diluted by the father. In every birth, unfortunately, there was always a father in the picture. In the case of her grandsons, she didn't know which boy was worse—the one related to her by blood or the one not. She decided she might take both boys out of her will as soon as she got home. David, who had the genes of her ancestors as well as hers and her husband's and Carol's, also carried the weird genes of his father, the madman who had killed himself with a vacuum hose and carbon monoxide from his car exhaust. No one Anna knew was acceptably related to her—not purely, not in a way she could tolerate. No one satisfied her but herself.

In a flood of indignation, she began to berate the boys despite Carol's warning look. "You children are hateful, disrespectful, rude, loud, and ungrateful." She hit them with her powerful vocabulary. "You are thoughtless, demanding, greedy, and inconsiderate." Then she added "Dirty." Then, "Filthy." Finally, directed at Abram, "Smelly."

Abram muttered something. Could Anna have heard right? With his handsome head bowed, could her grandson actually have said the unforgivable to her, *"Fuck off"*?

Anna thought she could possibly faint now that she had lived to see this day. She closed her eyes while the room spun. When she opened them, the Chanukah candles were lit, and Carol was reading from the side of the box the end of the prayer in English.

". . . Blessed art thou, O Lord our God, King of the Universe, who has kept us in life, and hast preserved us, and enabled us to reach this season . . ."

Preserved me too long, Anna thought. *Enough already.*

It was deadly quiet in the house. Carol had taken Abram to return the video tape to Leo's, and David had gone off to his bedroom and slammed the door. Only Mr. T and Anna were on the couch. Mr. T had his nose in Anna's lap, and she didn't have the strength to push him off. She already could feel fleas creeping up her arm.

She sat in the dark, with only the glow from the Chanukah candles lighting the room. She could try to have another talk with Carol when she came home, but what point would there be? Carol always took the boys' side. She had the same defense each time—"They've been deprived of enough as it is, Mom. They've had a very hard time. And they're no different from other kids their ages—thirteen and fifteen are very hard times, they're adolescents, they need to make noise, to release energy. They have very strong forces to deal with, peer pressure, their sex drives . . ."

"Don't fill me in with the details," Anna had said. "I watch Dr. Ruth. I know all about it."

She sat there, absently patting Mr. T. His tail thumped. At least with dogs, you could alter them, tone them down, defuse their energies. Anna wished she could alter the world, start over and give her daughter a good husband who could earn a living and wasn't crazy and wouldn't kill himself, give her two sons without anyone's genes at all, just two perfect respectful children, give her good health and a house out of the smog somewhere. And while she was at it, she'd bring Abram back for herself, and they'd take a condominium on the beach, also out of the smog.

Loud hammering came from David's room. What was he doing now? Knocking holes in the wall? She didn't have the

strength to go down the hall to see, not with the heavy cast
on her foot. But maybe she'd better. With his stupidity, who
knew what he was capable of?

"What's going on?" Anna said, opening his door. She
ignored a big sign that said, "KNOCK FIRST OR YOU'RE
DEAD."

"Nothing," David said. He was hammering small wooden
boards together on his desk.

"Don't tell me nothing when you're doing something. I'm
not blind and I'm not deaf, not yet," Anna said.

"I'm making a bed."

116   "You don't have a bed?"

"It's for my wrestler," David said.

"For who?"

"Hulk Hogan."

"Oh," Anna said. She was silent.

"Want to see him?" His voice, for once, was not a bark.

"Maybe . . ." Anna said.

David flung himself over his bed and pulled from beneath
it a shoe box. Inside, laid on tissue paper, covered with a
folded wash cloth, *tucked in*, was a miniature rubber thug,
Hulk Hogan, sleeping peacefully within the outlines of his
huge, ugly muscles.

"Want to hold him?" David asked. He offered her the
shoebox.

Anna stepped back. "Maybe later," she said. She was
touched by the vision of the doll. To think that David was
building a bed for that creature made her grandson seem
human, even sweet.

She left David hammering and wandered down the hall.
On Abram's door was the sign, "YOU'RE DEAD IF YOU
EVEN TOUCH THE DOORKNOB. DON'T BOTHER TO
KNOCK. *NO ONE* COMES IN HERE."

Anna pushed in the door. She expected the room to be a
shambles, a pigpen. But when she turned on the light, she
saw first the baseball cards, pinned in their plastic enve-

lopes in neat rows on the corkboard which lined one whole wall. Then she saw the airplane models, hanging on strings from the ceiling, silver fighter jets and brown vintage bombers, wafting in the draft from the heater vent. Abram's bed was made as tightly as a marine's. On his desk were a notebook and an open volume of the encyclopedia; Abraham Lincoln's face stared up at her from a photograph. It was clear her grandson had been working on some kind of report. Anna was having trouble breathing deeply. Not only could Abram the hoodlum maybe read, but he could also maybe write.

She carefully backed out of the room and closed the door.   **117**
In the TV room Mr. T had started barking violently. He ran from one end of the room to another, convulsed with hysterical yaps. David came out of his bedroom.

"I better go see what's up." His voice had suddenly become deep. "Someone might be in the yard." Boy and dog went outside through the patio door, and Anna found her way again to the couch, dragging her foot in its cast in the hospital-issue Abominable Snowman slipper. She heard Mr. T still yapping maniacally. David rushed inside and grabbed one of the burning Chanukah candles from the menorah, the one on top, the *shamesh*, and ran out again. "I need to see over the fence," he yelled. "Something bad is out there. Maybe a rat."

The next thing Anna saw through the plate glass window was an explosion. A flash of fire like an atom bomb. Then: David's screams.

She ran outside—she didn't know how she got there with her broken foot—to find her grandson on fire: there he was, huddled by the fence, a screaming flare of flame.

Don't, she commanded God. *Don't you dare do this.*

She found the hose, turned it on full, aimed it, tripped on the dog, saw stars overhead in the sky, found her balance, forced a Red Sea of water on his precious life. He was now down in the dirt; he knew to roll around on the ground, from television. She had seen him see that very scene on television on a murder mystery program. Thank God for television.

"Call 911! Call 911!" he yelled to Anna. That, too, from the movies. Last weekend Carol had rented *Down and Out in Beverly Hills*. Thank God for Hollywood. She pulled the wet child with her into the house and called 911.

When Carol and Abram came home, Anna and David were under a Charlie Brown quilt on the couch, watching a movie called *Pee Wee's Big Adventure*. David was in dry clothes and Anna was holding his hand; she was surprised at how huge it was, almost a man's hand. In the movie some daffy guy with a beanie on his head kept pedalling his bike backwards. David laughed everytime Pee Wee made a funny face, and when his body vibrated against Anna's chest, she laughed too.

"Should I tell them now?" David whispered into Anna's ear.

"Wait a few minutes. Let your mother get her breath." She touched David's face gently. His eyelashes had been singed off, but that was all. The paramedic had told Anna he would be fine. By some miracle, the Angel of Death had passed over the house like a silver jet.

But if it hadn't been Chanukah, David wouldn't have taken a candle out into the yard. If there hadn't been a can of charcoal lighter at the fence, he wouldn't have stood on it. If it hadn't tipped over, the cap wouldn't have come off. If the hot wax hadn't dripped down and ignited the charcoal lighter . . .

Well, never mind. If Anna had been born a Russian princess! If the world were square! If God were a kind man with a long beard!

Carol was busy in the kitchen unpacking bags of groceries. "I just stopped off to get a few more things we need," she called to her mother. Abram was standing by, yelling

118

"Neato" every time she unpacked an item that pleased him: a six-pack of Pepsi; frozen burritos; chocolate mint cream pie. When she pulled out bags of carrots, oranges, broccoli, he rolled his eyes and said, "Retch," accompanied by sound effects. Anna noticed that he was wearing new white tennis shoes after all. They had orange lightning bolts on them.

"Hey, David," Abram yelled into the dimness of the TV room. "Mom let me rent *Ghostbusters* again."

"Rad," David said, a little weakly. "Really rad."

"And we got another Heavenly Hash ice cream."

"Could we please have some over here before it's all gone?" Anna asked immediately. "With whipped cream if possible."

"Your wish is my command," Abram said. He danced around under the kitchen light like a boxer in his new shoes.

"But don't bring it to us yet. You help your mother unpack first," Anna said.

"And then we have something to tell you," David added. "It'll blow your mind."

119

THE LEAF LADY

The Leaf Lady was swirling her broom around on the cracked cement; no matter when Anna came up Granger Street, pulling her despised cart behind her, she saw the same angry woman, dressed in a blue bathrobe, jerking her yellow broom from side to side and daring the universe to dirty her sidewalk. Anna had no doubt that she was a landlady, probably as bad as her own.

A leaf came down. The Leaf Lady pounced, attacked it with a flurry of broomstraws, shunted it into her dustpan, delivered it triumphantly into her silver trash bag. Then she planted her feet apart, looked up, and waited for another to come down from the stunted, anemic tree.

Old ladies like this one gave a bad name to all old ladies. If Anna could be bumping along the street shaped like a beachchair or a candlestick or a rye bread, she would definitely prefer it to looking like this white-haired object in whose form she was housed. She glanced in the window of a car and winced at her reflection. Typical. The rounded shoulders, the delicate jowls, the fallen, sunken, loose skin of the face, the watery eyes. Even the ears on old people got huge, stretched out, as if to remind the world to speak up— more was needed, more of everything, if the old were to receive even a tiny bit of what used to be their due.

There was no point in trying to hide her age like some of the women at the Center did, with their platinum hairdos and their red-white-and-blue makeup. Besides, little things gave them away. In one second their stooped backs and their wire carts on wheels told the whole predictable story: osteoporosis and a dead husband. An army of women like Anna walked the streets. Who needed names or histories? You could guess a hundred life-stories and be right ninety-nine times: the one-room apartment, enough money in the bank to make up what Social Security didn't pay for, the big-shot children (at the Center, where Anna ate lunch every day, "movie producer" was the favorite; doctors, lawyers—they weren't so impressive any more).

Anna sighed with regret. In that department she was sorely lacking—her youngest daughter, Carol, was the widow of a lunatic who had killed himself (thank God, at least, for that) and her oldest, Janet, was married to a professor. Neither of her children was ever going to provide Anna with the key to a fancy condominium with soundproof walls. This was her heart's desire: to live in a place with no Armenians, no Russians, no gays, no babies, no aspiring musicians, no noises, no smells. And no landladies.

She dragged her cart down the curb and was nearly run down by a Mexican speeding by in an ancient red truck. And no Mexicans, she added. A warning flag flashed in her mind. These conveniences she wished for she would find soon enough in a hole in the ground. And for much cheaper than in a condominium. She shouldn't wish for something she wasn't ready for. Bernie, at the Center, warned everyone he met: "Don't have fancy wishes—God might make them come true."

God was a subject she wasn't going to get into now. She had to remember her shopping list. Although she wasn't superstitious—she didn't go hopping right now over to some tree to knock on wood that she had a good heart; she didn't spit to ward off the Evil Eye—she said aloud for the record, "For a hole in the ground I can wait a while."

She pulled her cart up the side of the far curb, grudgingly grateful that she had crossed Santa Monica Boulevard again and was still in one piece. Accidents were

122

the foe of old women. One day you were on your two feet, the next day you were in traction in a hospital room with some big-mouth who wouldn't shut up for five minutes.

Feeling she had crossed a wide, dangerous river, Anna glanced back across the street and saw the Leaf Lady watching her. She stared back. The old witch shook the top of her broom at her. She made shapes with her mouth. Anna guessed she was cursing and was not surprised. Everyone was crazy, and you couldn't make a friend in this world even if you wanted to.

In the Alpha Beta she got her coupons ready. Her fingers trembled as she put the flimsy bits of newspaper in order. Twelve cents off on orange juice, twenty-five cents off on a dozen eggs, fifty cents off on a pound of bacon. Nevermind that her sister Gert was outraged by Anna's fondness for bacon; when the Messiah came down personally to Anna and gave her one good reason why Abram had died so young, and *apologized*, then maybe she would consider giving up bacon. In the meantime she would eat what she liked.

She hooked her cart to the wire edge of the store's shopping wagon and began to push. The rubber wheels jammed and the steel bar caught Anna just under her breasts. The air went out of her. She stopped to wait for the pain to recede, and, as she stood there, a wagon crashed into her ankles. She cried out and spun around. A woman wearing a purple turban and a flowered pantsuit said, "Honey, this is no place to stand around daydreaming. This is heavy traffic."

"You should watch where you're going!"

"And *you* should go back to Russia where you belong!" the woman said, brandishing an armful of gold bracelets at Anna.

Russia! To be mistaken for a foreigner when she had been born in America!

"Oh go to hell," Anna said.

She gave a push on her wagon and got herself into the aisle with coffee and tea. Now came the business of comparing prices. She wasn't going to let them take her for a fool. One brand of coffee was eighteen-and-a-half cents an ounce, another was twenty-two cents an ounce. She would be here all morning if she had to, making calculations, but it was necessary.

She never even drank a whole cup of coffee. She made it for the warmth, for the smell, for the way the steam penetrated the china cup and heated her fingers. She always put in sugar and cream and let the aroma warm her cold face in the morning. She allowed herself this indulgence: to remember Abram every morning, the way he had enjoyed his breakfast, the two sunnyside-up eggs she fried for him, like happy eyes on his plate; how he wolfed down his toast, gulped his coffee. His appetites had been huge and wonderful.

She glanced up and thought she was having a stroke. Abram stood right next to her, as he would have looked if he'd grown old. He was in baggy gray pants, peering at boxes of teabags on the shelf next to the coffee. Oh—but he looked pathetic; his stretched-out brown sweater was pilled and stained, his shoes were scuffed and dusty, his wavy hair ragged. But he had the same hairline, the same bushy, down-slanted eyebrows, the crinkles around the good-natured eyes. Anna felt her heart skip and realized she had stopped breathing.

A miracle. Maybe she wouldn't buy bacon. She set her coupons down on the shelf and pretended to be examining a can of coffee. She glanced sideways at the man's shopping wagon. In it were six cans of Campbell's tomato soup. *God in heaven!* Like in her dream! In her dream, Abram was always in a shabby little room somewhere, without her, all alone, bent over his hot plate, heating up a can of tomato soup. There was a telephone in his room, an old black one, sitting like a squashed cross on a rickety wooden table. But in the dream she never knew the number, she could never reach him.

The man had Abram's large nose. He was shorter than Abram, but even men lose calcium, their spines shrink. All those years alone, twenty-three years alone in that room. What did he think about there? Her! He must think about Anna and the girls when they were little. Maybe even now, as he peered at the shelves in the Alpha Beta, he was thinking of her, the breakfasts she had made him, the pleasure she had given him. Tears flooded her eyes. *I'm all alone, too! I think of you every minute of my life!*

He selected Swee Touch Nee tea, the kind she always used, and she knew this was some kind of visitation. She reached out her hand, almost ready to pluck the sleeve of his sweater, to point herself out to him, but drew it back. The Anna he must remember was a young woman (only in her fifties!), whose face was still smooth, whose breasts (even then!) were like when she was sixteen. He was dreaming of his young wife; she was remembering her young husband, and here they stood, side-by-side, lives like pitchers that were tipped over and only a few drops left inside.

He took his tea and shuffled off behind his cart. Even the way his pants sank low on his hips was the same as Abram. But he was so shabby, so alone in the world, it broke her heart to see it. She made a sobbing sound and dug in her pocketbook for a handkerchief. She never carried on like this, but she had lost control. He was disappearing around the corner, going to the next aisle. She felt she had to hurry or he would be gone. She pushed hard against her cart, the wheels locked again, she was punched in the chest.

She sobbed openly as she struggled to push the wagon; it was like moving a mountain up the aisle. She turned the corner, knocking some bags of potato chips off a display. There he was! In front of frozen foods! Holding a pepperoni pizza in his hand, examining the pale, cheesy face of it.

125

Abram never ate a pizza in his life! Even when the girls first tasted it in high school, when they wanted the family to go out to dinner and eat it, he scorned it. Dough heavy as lead, he used to say. With cheese and meat mixed together! A horror, a disgusting invention.

Her senses returned to her. She let him go and turned her wagon the other way. What did she want him for anyway—a filthy old man who ate pizza, who now had an ugly frown on his face?

Her list, her shopping list. She had been here all this time and had bought nothing and was exhausted already. Her **126** chest ached, the backs of her ankles were scraped. And now . . . now she had lost her coupons! They were gone, not in her hand, not in her bag, not in her wagon. After she had scrupulously cut them out of the paper this morning, not one of them with a ragged edge so the checkout girl could complain, accuse Anna of sloppiness.

She began to retrace her steps, looking on the floor for her coupons. She wanted that fifty cents off on bacon. She was going to go home and cook half a pound for her dinner and eat it all at once, piece by piece, knowing it was from a pig, making it clear to God that she knew.

She found no coupons on the floor of the Alpha Beta. Anna walked slowly around the whole store, looking. She was about to give up when she spied an empty wagon by the bananas, just sitting there, abandoned. And in it were the same three coupons she had lost: for eggs, for bacon, for orange juice. The edges were ragged; someone less careful than she had torn them out of the paper. Whoever owned them must have got disgusted, as she often did. Couldn't find the juice. Didn't want to bother. The wagon didn't work and the person got fed up and walked out.

To test this assumption, Anna jiggled the wagon and felt the heavy locking of its rubber wheels. There—it was like a dead whale and it didn't happen just to her. But this person had been smart and just walked out. If more people did that, the Alpha Beta would wake up, oil their wheels.

She lifted the coupons out of the wagon and arranged them in her hand. She felt lucky. At least she could salvage something from this shopping trip. Maybe today would even turn out to be her lucky day. Maybe she would buy a lottery ticket when she checked out. What would she do with fifty thousand dollars? Buy a Steinway Grand. Buy two. Her spirits were beginning to revive.

"That's the woman!" a man yelled behind her just as she was picking up a package of bacon. "She's the one!" The old man, the Abram who wasn't Abram, was pointing his finger at her, an inch from her nose, and the woman in the purple turban and flowered pantsuit was running toward her, her face like a tornado.

"Did you steal my coupons?" she screamed, while the old man was blabbering, spit coming from his lips. "She took them right out of your wagon, I saw her!"

Anna waved the tattered coupons in the air. "Here! Take them! Who needs them? I thought someone left them there . . . no one was by the wagon . . . I had my own coupons, I brought them with me . . . I lost them."

"Yeah, yeah, yeah!" the woman said, tearing them from Anna's fingers. "Thief! I should have them call the police on you."

The old man, with his ugly, unfamiliar face, was glaring at her. His eyes were vicious.

Go eat your pepperoni! Anna thought. *Go to hell, all of you.*

She unhooked her little cart from the big wagon and dragged it toward the front of the store. She started out the IN door and it hit her in the face, opening automatically as someone approached it from outside.

Blindly, she backed away and found the other door, clattered out with her cart, crossed Santa Monica Boulevard. Cars honked and screeched around her. Let them run her over, she'd thank them.

The Leaf Lady looked up as Anna clanked her empty cart over the curb. She came to stand in the middle of the street, her robe gaping open, holding her broomstick like a spear. She pointed it at Anna's empty cart. "What's the matter?" she said. "There's nothing good enough for you in the whole store?"

"Oh drop dead," Anna said. She was crying and couldn't see where she was going.

"I wouldn't do you the favor," the Leaf Lady said. "Believe me, not even if it was the end of the world."

"If it was the end of the world, we'd all be better off," Anna said, moving right along.

"Not me," the Leaf Lady called after her. "I got property all over Venice."

"So I own two pianos," Anna yelled over her shoulder. "And even so, I say we'd be better off!"

"The kind of music you must play, maybe you're right!"

But Anna wasn't going to answer such stupidity. She dragged her wagon homeward, watching out for potholes.

128

MOZART YOU
CAN'T GIVE THEM

In the downstairs apartment the young Mexican boy began to knock his head against the wall. Sometimes Anna thought it was just the low bass beat of some tenant's stereo, but as soon as she realized it wasn't regular, she knew it was the boy starting his morning tantrum. At least if he had some sense of rhythm—a little drummer boy. But he wasn't musical, only crazy. At almost the same instant the Russian lady across the courtyard began playing violent streaks of dissonance on her cello. Immediately Anna pictured a blackboard, wide and colorless as Russia, and across it came the shrieking chalk, an empty train scraping and grinding its way over the bleak plains. The woman should have stayed in Russia where there was more space, and not moved here to live ten feet from Anna and give her a headache every day.

As if all that weren't enough, Anna heard the clatter of the barbecue lid being lifted outside, and she rushed to lock her windows. On the tiny balcony next to Anna's, the father of the Armenian family was lighting the barbecue starter again. What was wrong with these people that they had to cook three times a day over charcoal? Didn't they know how to use a stove? If they were civil human beings in the first place, she would tell them that this kind of cooking could give them cancer. But when she slammed the sliding glass door shut, the man always sneered at her, looking like a walrus with his hanging mustache, and threw more lighter on the coals, for spite.

Charred edges of meat, which tasted like heaven itself, could kill you. What couldn't kill you? Pickled herring could kill you, lox could kill you, everything was full of nitrites. Anna heard plenty of lectures at the Senior Citizens' Center, she was an informed woman. Chicken fat could kill you, cream cheese, sour cream, bacon; for years these foods had tempted her to stay alive. When her sister Gert had come with her to the Center for the lecture by the nutritionist, bacon had been the day's main subject. The old man Bernie, who was at the Center all the time, announced that if you drank orange juice when you ate bacon, something in the juice would cancel out the cancer. Gert had poked Anna and muttered, "Jews—all of these Jews—they have no business eating bacon anyway. No business even *talking* about it!"

"Look, get modern, will you?" Anna had said to her. "Get with the twentieth century. You're still living back in the horse-and-buggy age."

"At least people were decent then," Gert had insisted. "Not like this sewer we live in now. Don't invite me to any more lectures. I'm better off at home."

The fumes from the Armenians' patio were filling Anna's apartment, choking her. "Who needs the Gestapo when you have this?" She dragged her kitchen chair into the walk-in pantry closet and closed the door, sitting there in the dark with the matzo meal boxes and the cans of soup. The stink of the charcoal lighter filled every crevice. "What should I do?" she said aloud into the darkness. "Run away three times a day to walk up and down Santa Monica Boulevard till they finish their steaks? Get myself mugged while they eat like horses on my tax money? They should only choke." She hoped the charred meat would work fast on them.

What had *happened* to America, anyway? After seventy-five years of running away from the East Side of New York with all those barbarians, here she was again with *these*. No progress. All that culture she thought was out there in the world, that she had tried to absorb, came to nothing—to this. What did the world care that Anna Goldman lived in two rooms, and in each room she had a piano!

There was a thud against the wall of the closet. She felt she had been hit in the kidneys.

"Wally, I swear—I'll bite off your little finger if you ever do that again!"

Another thud. The gay young men next door. She knew their pattern. A loud yelling fight, full of accusations. Dishes breaking. Furniture sliding around. Then the lengthy reconciliation, with those noises! Worse than cats in heat. Wasn't it embarrassing for them to meet her at the trash bin after they had carried on like that? Howls, gasps, shrieks, moans! *"Oh my God, oh my God, oh my God,"* one of them always screamed a hundred times. They should only do it in a church where God could hear them, Anna thought, and give me some peace. But when she met one or the other of them at the garbage bin, so well-groomed in his pink silk shirt, or his net underwear, he'd always graciously lift the lid for her, toss her garbage into the back, where she couldn't reach, wish her a good day. At least those boys had manners. They were raised in good American families. But she wouldn't go so far as to let them pull her grocery cart up the steps to her apartment. The last thing she needed was AIDS. She had read in the *LA Times* about the bathhouses in San Francisco, the catwalks where men would stand so others could do a specialized activity on them. Well, that was their business. She was modern, live and let live. Not like Gert, out of the dark ages. But did she have to listen to it all day? She had stopped eating out altogether except for the Center because so many of those gay boys worked in the restaurants. They had a knack for cooking. But did she want them laying lettuce on her tuna sandwiches? Not after where those hands had been!

131

She opened the closet door; the fumes enclosed her and she could almost feel the flames on her skin, crisping it like bacon.

"Bastards," she whispered. In her old age she should come to this, locked in a closet, instead of revered, respected, with her children gathered round. "They have their own lives to live," she corrected herself. They were loving and loyal, her daughters called her every day. She didn't want to live near them, the way Gert urged her to do—live in the suburbs with a church on every corner and listen to the leaf-blowers blast out her eardrums. The expert on high blood pressure at the Center had lectured on how noise raises the blood pressure of rats within two hours. He should only be here today listening to the racket from the Russian's apartment—he would have a stroke in five minutes.

"Enough of the dark," she said. She stepped out of the closet and heard her doorbell shrilling.

"Who is it?" she yelled, standing ten feet back from the door.

"It's only your landlady, darling, it's not a mugger. Open the door, Mrs. Goldman—we have something to talk about here."

Bitch face Anna thought. *I am not in the mood for this now.* She unlocked her three locks and drew the chain back. "I was just going out, Mrs. Blungman. I give a concert today. Can you make it fast?"

"At our age you shouldn't be in such a hurry," she said, "or it could kill you one-two-three." Mrs. Blungman was short and fat, like a matzo ball. Her face was a lump of dough, with a nose plopped on, two eyes gouged out, and cold blue marbles pressed in the holes. Her hair was thin, like white cotton thread pasted on a child's pink rubber ball.

"I have a complaint against you."

"Who made it?" Anna demanded.

"My sources are confidential. By the way, could it be it was you picked a lemon from my lemon tree?"

"Of course not! Why would I take one of your precious lemons?"

"Lemons are very expensive now in the stores."

"For your information, Mrs. Blungman, I could afford to pay a *dollar* for a lemon if I had to."

"So it wasn't you?"

"So I said."

"So, now to the complaint."

"That wasn't the complaint?"

"The complaint is coming, don't worry, it's right here on my tongue."

133

"Make it fast please. I'm on my way out."

"Alone? You of all people should know how dangerous these streets are. Where's your head after being held up at gunpoint in your store! You take big risks, Mrs. Goldman."

"When I'm in the tomb I won't take risks," Anna said.

"You don't sweep your patio," said Mrs. Blungman.

"I don't sweep my patio? You send spies up to my patio? It's two feet by two feet—I never go out there. No one can see it. The sun never shines there. It stinks from the Armenians' barbecue. I pay rent for my privacy. My patio is my kingdom just like my bathroom."

"So—since you raised the subject yourself, I wasn't going to discuss that today—I would like to know how come there are scratches in your toilet bowl? You clean it with Brillo? We don't allow that."

Anna felt her blood bubble up through her veins.

"You go snooping in my toilet? That's illegal. I could sue you."

"It's legal, darling, for a landlord to have a key to every apartment, in case of fire, to paint, to fix the air conditioner."

"You haven't painted in five years. The air conditioner has been broken since I moved in . . ."

Mrs. Blungman cut her off. "And we could evict you, Mrs. Goldman, if you don't keep your windows open from now on. Because for some crazy reason you keep them all locked up when you go out, and that causes termites in the building."

"That's ridiculous! That's insane! You're the one who's crazy! Termites if I close my windows!" Anna began to close the door. Mrs. Blungman stopped her with a heavy hand.

"I didn't get to the main complaint yet, darling."

"Your time is up. I have to go somewhere."

134 "They don't like your piano playing in the next building."

"Who says so?"

"I got sources. Not every apartment would allow two pianos for one tenant. You have twenty fingers?"

"I told you—one is from the antique store. When I had to give it up, I took the piano from the store here. But I only play one piano at a time. And with the soft pedal, always."

"The people in the next building don't like what you play."

"What? You want me to submit a program to them for approval?"

"You play too gloomy. If they have to listen they would like a few show tunes, a patriotic march, something from Barbra Streisand. Not what you give them."

"Mozart you can't give them," Anna said. "Of this I am aware."

"You live on a high horse, Mrs. Goldman. Relax a little, enjoy."

"As long as I sweep my patio and clean my toilet."

"You got it, darling."

Anna walked toward the Senior Citizens' Center. The streets swarmed with foreigners. She could be anywhere— Korea, Israel, Mexico, China. English was no longer the main language of this country. Even on Fairfax Avenue, Yiddish was getting buried. She would go into a bakery, and the women working there were wearing babushkas and jabbering in Russian. She would go to the doctor's office, and the technicians told jokes in Spanish. On top of this, the respectful separation of the sexes was gone—to have a cardiogram she had to submit to a black man snapping his fingers as he plopped rubber suction cups around the edges of her breasts. Her poor misled father, with his dreams of coming to America where the streets were paved with gold. Where anyone could become president (but not a Jew, he realized before he died young). He worked so hard, sewing all day in the factories, bringing home piecework at night. But here the foreigners came with jewelry hidden in their underwear, took their doles from the government, and broiled steaks on their barbecues while Anna choked. The foreigners thought life was a big joke—they were always laughing on the streets. Israeli men wearing gold chains in layers around their hairy necks pushed their dark-eyed, round-nosed babies up and down the streets in fancy strollers. In the city college where Anna took classes, the students with their slanty eyes or their gold-toned skin or their peasant faces all seemed slack, tired, indifferent. Their grades were barely C's. None of them were like the immigrants she was descended from. *They* had worked like demons, learning the language, learning the ways of the new world. These people came and had it handed to them. They came to America poor, but they wouldn't work hard. They wouldn't learn English.

A few years ago when Anna had had her surgery, the Filipino nurses in the hospital had joked in their jabbering tongue, right over her head as if she were nothing more than a tree trunk in the bed, completely ignored her as they wired her into the transfusion machinery; they gossiped nonstop, joked—didn't have the proper respect for their work, for life and death, and for patients who were fighting

135

for one over the other. They thought it was just a big party over here, that's all.

Anna didn't care, as Gert did, about morals, wasn't horrified by the prostitutes strutting up and down Hollywood Boulevard, or by the gay men screaming *oh my God* at their heights of passion. Sex was one thing. She could live with it if she had to, as long as no one was seducing her. But laziness, pure greed and laziness, that was something else.

"Where you been keeping yourself all my life, Sweet Lips?"

136 "I have no patience for you today, Bernie," Anna said, taking her tray, and moving along the lunch line. She only came to the Center because if she ate a real meal at lunchtime (and who could deny that seventy-five cents was a good price?) she wouldn't have to worry about cooking anything for her dinner. She weighed just under a hundred pounds—a fact which was both a source of pride and worry. If she should catch the flu, and not be able to eat for a week, she had no margin to depend on, she would turn into a skeleton. But compared to the matzo-ball ladies all over the place, she had the edge—a certain grace, a swing of her skirt. Bernie wasn't the only one after her. She could see herself in the mirror behind the cafeteria workers—her white hair perfectly short, clipped in a clean, even line. Not a single curl, a pompadour, a frizz; not a bleached mop, not a wig, not a movie-star's head of hair on the face of a crone. Integrity was what she stood for. She was a lost soul, one of a kind, and no one cared about what she stood for.

"White meat of the chicken, please," Anna said.

"Take what's on the plate or leave it, darling," the woman said. "You don't get special privileges."

"Listen, you *know* me," Anna said. "I volunteer my time at this Center just like you, I play a concert here every week. Today in fact."

The woman shoved the plate at her. Diamonds sparkled

on her fingers. "A leg and a wing, darling—that's what's on this plate. Take it or leave it."

Bitch face Anna thought. Give them a little authority and they become like prison wardens. Mrs. Blungmans were everywhere. Sadistic. Vicious. The human race was too far gone. This woman was one of the worst, with her airs and her Zsa-Zsa accent.

Bernie sat next to her. His hands shook as he spread his napkin across his stained gray pants-legs. "My offer is still good, Angel Face," he said, beginning to lift a forkful of peas to his mouth. By the time he got the fork halfway up, most of the peas had spilled off. Anna brushed a pea angrily from her skirt. **137**

"We'll take a cruise to Europe, just you and me, first-class, we'll dance the night away, Emerald Eyes."

She'd been through this before. She'd had a vision of herself in the middle of the ocean, with his corpse on the bed and the band playing "God Bless America" in the grand ballroom. ("A millionaire wants to marry me," Anna had told her daughters. "He has no children—you girls could be rich." "Don't sell your soul for us," the girls had advised her. "Don't worry," Anna had replied. "I wouldn't dream of it.")

The creamed corn was like glue. The chicken leg had a bone showing through, jagged, with black blood clotted in its marrow. Anna reached for her milk carton; her thumbs pressed the edges back and pain shot into both her elbows. She clamped her teeth and waited for it to pass. She didn't need reminders from her nerve endings of what was going on inside her.

"You're doing the wrong end," Bernie said, grease on his chin. "Here, I'll do it for you, Sweet Lips."

She pushed the carton toward him. Bernie couldn't open the milk container either. He was struggling intently, his tongue showing, breathing loudly, pulling at the cardboard with his gnarled fingers. Anna felt her mouth turn down, and tears, like burning acid rising too high from her empty stomach, seared her eyes.

She stood up. Her lunch lay congealing on the paper plate. She touched Bernie on the shoulder, gently.

He didn't turn his head to look up at her; he had arthritis of the neck bones. "I'll be down at the rec room at your concert, Gorgeous," he said. "I'll be there in ten minutes, front row, center. You'll know me by the red rose in my lapel."

138 In the bathroom Anna combed her hair and saw in the mirror her father's dream—the girl with long sugar-water curls, the girl raised up in the land of opportunity who could play so beautifully the piano he had worked for years to buy her. He wouldn't know her now if he saw her. The skin of her face was an accordion of the days of her life, folded one upon the other. This was what was left of her. What counted was inside, invisible.

Carrying her music, swinging her skirt, she went down the long empty hall to the rec room. The piano keys had only half their ivories. The keyboard welcomed her with its toothless grin.

She knew what they liked, her ten or twelve regulars and the four or five other poor souls who wandered into the rec room, passing time till the free blood pressure test or the cholesterol lecture. They liked "Fiddler on the Roof," "The Entertainer," "Roll Out the Barrel." She knew: *Mozart you can't give them*—but this was her show. It might do them some good. She opened her music book and warmed up her fingers.

THE
BLOOD PRESSURE BUNCH
AND THE
ALZHEIMER'S GANG

At the Multi-Purpose Center there was a bigger crowd for Anna's concert than usual; free blood pressure readings started in an hour—this allowed time for the sediment of the subsidized lunch to settle. The old folks were shuffling their way into the rec room like a herd of cows. Lowing and mooing, scrambling for seats, they were giving their own concert, a regular barnyard symphony—what did they need Anna for?

She ran a few scales up and down the keys of the old spinet; it was badly out of tune, but what did they know— these peasants and barbarians who came to hear her. When the scraping of canes and the whirring of wheel chairs had quieted, she played a few bars of the theme from *Dragnet* to get everyone's attention. Then she swung around on the bench.

"Ladies and gentlemen"—she was as cordial as their round vacant cow-eyes would permit—"today I will be playing a program of Beethoven, Mozart, and Chopin."

A crackling noise in the first row directed Anna's attention to an old man in a wheel chair who was burrowing intently in a brown paper bag in his lap. "Excuse *me*," Anna said. He extracted a bagel which he held up to the light, examining it for defects. "Sir, the lunch hour is over. I ask that no eating take place during the concert."

He appeared not to hear her.

"I just *loathe* Beethoven," said a loud voice from somewhere in the back. This took Anna's breath away. She searched unbelievingly for a face in this room which knew enough to speak the word *loathe.*

"Who said that?" she demanded. "Who?"

"Me." A frizzy blonde, wearing green pants and a pink blouse, stood up. "Beethoven you could die of from boredom. Can't you do a nice tune from *Chorus Line?*"

"I don't know *Chorus Line,*" Anna said. "Sit down please."

The woman stared at her. "You don't know *Chorus Line?* It's only been the biggest hit on Broadway for the last fifty years!"

"I don't specialize in Broadway," Anna said. "Would you please sit down so we can get started?"

"Yeah, sit down!" Bernie yelled. Anna's buddy: he winked at her four times. Or maybe it was the tic from his neuralgia. "Sit down or you get bounced out of here."

Anna waited. She made it clear she would stand there till they behaved. What could she expect in the way of decorum, manners, taste? They were from the jungle. Even when Anna went to the Music Center to hear the greats, the audience applauded at the wrong time—at the end of a movement, sometimes even at a rest in the music. Right in front of her at this very moment, the old man in the wheelchair—could a person believe this?—was smearing his bagel with cream cheese from a little paper cup balanced on his knee.

"You," Anna said. "The gentleman right here. *You! There is no eating allowed in this room.*"

"Oh—give him a break," the blonde in the pink blouse yelled. "He came too late for lunch, they wouldn't let him in. So let him have his little snack."

The man was chewing quite happily. He smiled at Anna, gratefully, sweetly, his eyes bright. Like a little monkey, he looked at her from under his bushy eyebrows. All right, he was from the Alzheimer's Gang, he didn't know any better.

Anna swung back around on her seat and brushed her hands delicately over her skirt. She positioned her hands and began to play the first notes of the "Moonlight Sonata." Immediately a scuffling started up behind her; she threw a fast look over her shoulder.

"What is this?" she cried, stopping at once.

"Play, honey, play," said a woman of no less than ninety years. She was spinning around on the floor. "You make my heart happy. When do I ever get a chance to dance like this?" She waltzed in a circle by herself, holding a bulging shopping bag against her chest.

Anna looked around to see if there was someone, anyone, who could understand her exasperation with a lunatic like this. But all of them had the same blank innocent eyes— cows chewing their cud. There was no way to get respectful attention here. No way at all.

"Please, please!" Anna said. "Sit down. If you want to dance, join the dance class."

"I'm all done, darling," the old woman said. "My breath is gone. My pacemaker only lets me celebrate a few seconds at a time. So don't worry, I'm all done. Relax. Sit down now and play some more, send us to seventh heaven."

Anna Goldman and Arthur Rubinstein were the only two people in the world who knew what a battle it was to get the attention of the mindless masses.

"The piano has a little look of a coffin," Rubinstein said a few years ago on the *MacNeil-Lehrer Report*. At home Anna had a typed copy (she sent away two dollars to the television station) of what Rubinstein had said in the interview. She kept it on her coffee table and read it every day for support. Arthur would certainly sympathize with her right now if he were here. He knew how hard it was, he said it himself: how people came to listen to him play after a good dinner, the women thinking only about dresses, the men about business or sports. *"There I have this crowd, not really knowers of music . . . and that is a very difficult*

*proposition. I have to hold them . . . by my emotion . . .
there is a moment where I please them all . . . I can hold
them with one little note in the air, and they will not
breathe. . . . That is a great, great moment. Not always
does it happen, but when it does happen, it is a great
moment of our lives."*

Well, it didn't ever happen at the Multi-Purpose Center.
Anna wished Arthur Rubinstein were her husband. She
would leave here and go home, and there he'd be on her
little worn-out couch, waiting for her, sipping tea, listening
to music in his head. She would tell him about the crazies at
her concert, and he'd commiserate, nod his head, say,
"Well, you're doing them good, music is good for their
souls." He would think they had souls. She didn't.

She really *could* have married him. He was born in 1887,
only twenty years before she was. She could have met him,
they would have had brilliant children, great musicians.
Not that she hadn't loved her Abram, not that she didn't
love her girls, but her musical gene had been diluted to
nothing in her children by Abram, a sweet man but not an
artist, a man who couldn't play a note. The girls didn't turn
out to have one drop of musical talent. When they were
little she would threaten them: "I'm going to swallow iodine
if you don't sit down and practice." She and Arthur
Rubinstein had the same passionate nature—they were
both from Polish stock. Like Anna with her iodine, he had
tried to kill himself when he was twenty because he had no
money and he was in love with a married woman who
wouldn't get a divorce. Hanging himself didn't work—the
things he used broke—so he sat down and played the piano
instead. Anna understood this exactly; that's what she always did. When it became clear to her (which it did every
day) that life was all a big nothing, she sat down and played
the piano. So here she was: playing for the Blood Pressure
Bunch and the Alzheimer's Gang.

She surrendered herself to the notes of the "Moonlight
Sonata" and pretended Rubinstein was watching her from

142

the poster on the wall that said "High Blood Pressure Is the Silent Killer"—he was listening to her, his beautiful long head cocked slightly to the side. She closed her eyes, feeling the pedals rise and fall under her feet. She had a sense of herself as a ballerina, lightly moving over a green meadow. Rubinstein was admiring the way her delicate shoulders swayed, the way her girlish waist bent, the airy movement of the hem of her skirt. Her face, her ancient, fallen face, was bowed over the keys, hidden from view. Even her hands, whose skin was as crinkled and brown as the bag which held the old man's bagel, moved like graceful white birds. All that she was was in the music.

"Bravo, Passion Flower!"

Oh, shut up, Bernie!

"Come to my tent tonight!" he called.

Men and their circulating hormones. They never gave up. Even Rubinstein was probably dreaming of it when he was ninety-five. Abram had looked forward to it, every night if she would let him, not really believing that the next day she always had a migraine. Even when she had a migraine, and told him so, he'd say, "I'll make it better. I'll kiss it away." Beethoven probably had it on his mind all the time, too. Otherwise, how could he write music like this? The calm after the struggle, the peace in the moonlight.

When it was over, when she had grudgingly played "Sunrise, Sunset" as her encore, she began to gather up her music.

"That was very good, I want you to know you have talent," the blonde in the green pants said to Anna. "Would you be interested in a blind date? You look like you could use a little social life."

"I look somehow lacking to you?" Anna asked. The woman had wrists and ankles like an ox, a peasant face.

"You look good for your age, you kept your weight down," the woman said.

"Thank you."

"The man I have in mind for you is my neighbor. He's in the hospital now with his prostate. But a wonderful musician. When he gets out is what I'm thinking—he used to play the tuba in the Cleveland Symphony before his emphysema."

"He'll need a nurse when he gets out," Anna said.

"So—what's the harm if you make a little chicken soup till he's on his feet? This is a wonderful man I'm talking about, a prize."

"If he's so wonderful, why don't you have a social life with him?"

144 "I'm dating a butcher, thank you," she said. "Kosher. The finest cuts of meat."

"Meat at our age is very bad," Anna said. "Don't you listen at the lectures? And will you please excuse me now?" Anna said. "I'm very tired."

"He would appreciate your thin hips. His wife, she should rest in peace, was a hippopotamus down there."

"Excuse me," Anna said. "I'm not feeling well."

"It's the food they serve us here. Surplus from World War Two, I think."

Bernie was now closing in on her; she had the impression that he was flapping his lips like a goldfish.

"Look!" Anna pointed to the door. "They're lining up for blood pressure! You two don't want to miss it. High blood pressure is the silent killer."

Anna sat at her kitchen table and ate a chocolate chip cookie. No Arthur Rubinstein was on her couch. It was getting dark and the gay boys next door were playing "The Tennessee Waltz." Her daughters were probably cooking dinner in their houses, something warm and nourishing, possibly even stuffed cabbage, which it seemed to her she had last made in another life. Her girls—an hour away in the suburbs—always said, "We wish you lived nearby, then you could have dinner with us." They didn't know what they were saying. If she lived nearby, there would be no end of complications. For example, Janet's husband, the professor, had a habit of chewing his applesauce. This annoyed Anna and she would probably have to say something eventually. Her other son-in-law had had much worse habits—and to him she had said plenty—but he was dead. She sometimes thought she should move in with Carol and help her raise the boys.

Neither of the boys could spell the simplest words; they had never even *heard* of Beethoven—all they cared about was some ugly gorilla called Hulk Hogan. Also, they devoured food like King Kong. They lived—like some new mutation of penguins—in the refrigerator. Whenever Anna looked at them, two healthy boys, they always had an arm stuck in the freezer, pulling out frozen pizzas, frozen burritos, frozen donuts, and always—the other hand wrapped around a can of soda, as if milk didn't exist. They had things in and out of the microwave so fast, it was like watching a speeded-up film. Anna was appalled to see that much food disappear down their gullets. No one needed to eat that much, that constantly. She was sure most of it passed out of their systems undigested. And their mother let them get away with it. It was true Carol had other things on her mind; she had to devote a great deal of time going to singles' events and then getting depressed from the losers she met, but still . . .

There was no point trying to run her children's lives. From a distance, it was all right to see their flaws and get annoyed; if she lived with them, she would probably have a stroke every day from their stupidity. Maybe what she needed to take her mind off her troubles was a social life. But did she want a blind date with an invalid tuba player who had been married to a hippopotamus?

If only Rubinstein were eligible! If only money grew on trees and everyone were a genius! If Anna decided to go looking among the hordes, she would have to be very

145

choosy. She'd seen an interesting ad in the personal column in the paper for the last three weeks. She had it right here on the table:

"Scrabble Expert welcomes challenge from Smart Cookie. Former Navy officer with medals, now senior citizen; owns seventeen dictionaries. Non-smoking gentleman. Wordsmith. Elocution afficionado. Will come to you. Or vice-versa. Call 653-1050."

At least here was a man who knew a word or two. These days, even that was a miracle.

146   "I'm rapturous that you called, you sound very intelligent," the man said on the phone. "You want to elucidate and maybe give your name?"

"Not yet. I don't reveal my name to strangers so fast," Anna said.

"You want your nomenclature to be 'Hey you'?"

"Slow down," Anna said. "You live alone?"

"A widower for ten years, tired of solitary hibernation. I have impressive references if you want; I'm clean living, no drinking, no gambling. My late wife was an angel; I respect women, believe me, so I'm not looking for funny-business."

"What are you looking for?"

"Companionship, a good game of Scrabble, maybe a steak dinner out now and then."

"Steak is a death sentence at our age," Anna said. "You're how old?"

"A young seventy-three. And you?"

"Around there," Anna said. "In very good shape."

"You have a pencil? I'll give you directions."

"How could you imagine I would come to a perfect stranger's house? How do I know you have honorable intentions?" On the last words Anna's voice had turned coy and flirtatious, which astonished her—that such a tone still lived within her.

"That's very perspicacious of you. I respect caution these

days. So let me get a pencil—you'll give me directions to your place."

"What about your seventeen dictionaries—you carry them with you?"

"On the bus that would be foolish."

"I'm thinking suddenly this is a mistake," Anna said. "Nice as I'm sure you are, I can't let a perfect stranger come to my house."

"If I'm perfect, what's the worry?"

Anna was silent. She considered hanging up.

"I'm sorry," he said. "A bad choice of a joke."

"I'll think about this and call you in a few days."

147

"No! Don't hang up! Please! Let's not lose this propitious event."

"You don't have many calls on your ad?"

"Not from a cultured, charming person with expertise like yourself, who sounds like twenty years old."

"All right," Anna said. "I have an idea. We could meet at the Multi-Purpose, you know the one on Fairfax?"

"Certainly I do. Tomorrow?"

"I could arrange it. After lunch. In the lobby. One o'clock."

"I'll bring Scrabble."

"Good," Anna said.

"So now, would you consider it wise to tell me your name?"

"Anna Goldman."

"How do you do, Anna?"

"And you go by . . .?"

"Jack . . . Jack or Izzy Fine, take your pick, what suits your inclinations."

"Thank you," Anna said. "Jack is fine."

"I'll count the minutes, already my stopwatch is running," he said.

Anna laughed in spite of herself. Then she carefully lowered her voice and said goodbye sternly. Still, the instant she hung up, she laughed out loud again. For the briefest moment, everything in her kitchen looked bright, as if little lights had gone on inside her teapot, her sugar bowl, and her toaster oven.

But when she actually saw him in the lobby, spiffy in a sport jacket, his two strands of white hair glued to his spotted brown scalp, her throat closed. She knew him by the Scrabble set in his lap. But aside from that, she knew him. By his high waist, by his thin legs, by his flabby arm muscles. She knew him the same way she knew the legions of old ladies—she knew his story: the dead wife, the kids (he'd have complaints about them or he'd rave about how good they were to him). Either he was lonely, or he had ten old ladies making propositions of marriage every day. Or not *even* of marriage—of anything! There were eighty-five women for every fifteen decrepit, on-their-last-legs old men in this town, and most of them were shameless!

Anna wobbled forward on her high heels toward the row of orange chairs, one of which contained Jack Fine. She could break an ankle from this vanity. The smell of the perfume she had sprayed on her neck was choking her. Her skirt had little gold threads woven through it which caught the ceiling lights and flashed reflections up at her to give her the symptoms she'd been warned about by Dr. Rifkin: the way it would feel when her retina detached. Her blind date was sitting rigid, clutching a battered brown Scrabble box. His tie, bright red, dotted with white anchors, was knotted so high under his chin it appeared to be cutting off his air. His face was mottled with matching red circles—probably a symptom of impending stroke. She could tell he was wearing a laundry-starched shirt to impress her. A gold tie clasp gleamed. She had a vision of him taking off his shirt; in fact, he was suddenly taking off all his clothes right in front of her. They were perhaps already married—or, if she had lowered her standards, maybe going on a cruise together.

148

But there she was, stuck with him. His spine was sunken between the white slack muscles of his curved back. And the rest—God help her! She didn't want to *imagine* the rest of what she'd see if he took off his pants!

And in between now and the fabulous cruise—the eternity of dinners with him, his false feeth digging into steak after steak! The earliest confiding conversations: which operations he had had, which she had had, which ones he needed, which ones she needed. And the ailments yet to come for both of them! They would never run out of material.

But finally, and most terrifying, as they progressed into **149** their future together, he would have to get it over with. "Play the piano for me, Anna," he would ask, because, if he was any kind of gentleman, if he was decent, he'd have to recognize "her interests." He would lean back on her couch, chivalrous, gallantly stifling his yawns while she was coerced into betraying Mozart for him!

Not a moment too soon she stopped to scrutinize a cholesterol poster: a dead cow and a happy fish. Her beloved Arthur Rubinstein had said that people who think happiness is to enjoy a good cutlet and go to bed and win at a game are stupid. *"There is nothing in it,"* he had said. *"That is not life. Life is bite into it, to take absolutely as it is."*

Jack Fine, a sailor's sappy grin hanging crooked on his face, was sweeping the field with his lighthouse eyes. His beam hit her square in the face and knocked her off course. One second more and Anna might not have escaped. Now it was merely a matter of deserting him at dockside. All right—it wasn't the most refined thing to do, but it wouldn't be such a horror. He'd sit there alone for maybe ten more minutes. By then a half-dozen dames would be closing in, complimenting the anchors on his tie.

COMES AN
EARTHQUAKE
. . . .

Anna—who never once played a card game in her adult
life—leaned back in one of the red metal chairs furnished
for the guests of the Colby Plaza and watched her sister Ava
hunched over her cards. Anna had been in Miami Beach
five days already and was still at a loss to understand Ava
and her friends. Furred in mink stoles and intent on their
hands, they expertly slid new cards into their fans, closing
and opening them like magic. What Anna couldn't understand was how these old ladies—women who'd lived
through the Depression, who'd lost sons in the war (Ava's
son went down over New Guinea and her youngest boy was
peppered with shrapnel in France), women who'd lost a
husband or two—could just sit on their behinds eight hours
a day on a porch in Miami Beach and play poker!

"I'm wondering . . ." Anna said, "how is it that no one
around here ever walks to the beach, only a block away?
Where I live, in Los Angeles, you could give your right arm
for a breath of air like this."

"So why not move here?" asked one of the ladies. No one
raised her head from over her cards; Anna wasn't sure if
the voice belonged to Ida (whose husband, Herman, was
upstairs with Alzheimer's) or Sadie (emphysema—she
smoked four packs a day) or Ava's best friend, Mickey (her
husband had had a fatal heart attack when he tripped on
two gay boys, naked on the beach at night, a year ago).

"Why should anyone move to a morgue?"

A man's voice. At first Anna thought it came from Collins
Avenue, from the sidewalk five feet in front of her chair
where a trickle of old folks passed by in the deepening
dusk. The women, dragged down by their diamonds and
mink, promenaded, as if along a hospital corridor, on the
arms of old men wearing jackets and bow ties. Anna
glanced along the row of metal chairs till she made out what
looked like a dark balloon floating against the pink stucco
of the hotel wall. She tried to focus her eyes. Glaucoma was
working its way through her retina; one of these days the
sights of the world would go black on her. (Amazing, how
152 this morning, Ava, needing to sew a button on her house-
coat, threaded the needle in just one pass; eyes like an eagle
and she was ninety to Anna's seventy-eight.)

"Irving bubbie, light of my life, go back upstairs or go
across to the Crown and see the show but do us a favor and
shut up," said Sadie.

"Aah, they die like flies here," Irving said. "What's the
point? Tell me," he leaned forward and addressed Anna.
"What is the point of it all?"

Anna squinted, trying to see him better. She made out a
pair of white suede loafers with red rubber soles, some
skinny knees.

"There *is* no point," Anna said in his direction. "You're
right—it's all a big nothing."

"Look around you," he said. "We all come to the last stop
like lemmings running to the ocean. We run to Miami Beach
and play cards with our last breaths. We're dying and
playing cards at the edge of the cliff till we get shoved off."

"You're a sick man?" Anna asked.

"I have AIDS," he said.

"AIDS?" Anna said, shocked. She shut her mouth tightly.
He didn't look like the type, but you could never tell. A
snort came from Ava at the card table.

"Tell her, Irving, what kind of AIDS you have."

"You want to know?" He addressed Anna.

"Don't feel you have to talk about it," she said, trying to breathe very shallowly.

"I'm happy to tell you. I'm able to talk very freely about this." He paused. "I got hearing aids!"

It took a moment for Anna to digest this information. Then she felt taken. She wished fervently she were home in her dark apartment in Los Angeles where the Armenians next door choked her with their barbecue fumes. She had come on this trip to Florida to see Ava one last time before one of them died. Sisters were sisters, after all, and how much time was there? Ava already had a pacemaker and an artificial heart valve. Anna, thank God, had only the usual: arthritis, glaucoma, osteoporosis, high blood pressure, nothing serious.

153

Irving said, "If you don't laugh, you'll cry, take your pick."

"Serious things like AIDS you shouldn't joke about," Anna insisted. "Have some respect."

"For what? I should take the world seriously? Why should I? What's the world ever given me that's any good except maybe my children?"

"And then even they don't visit," Anna remarked strictly for his benefit only, since her daughters, when she was home in LA, called her every day.

"Not *my* children. My daughter is married to a millionaire," Irving corrected Anna. "She sends a limousine for me every Sunday, I go to eat Chinese, Italian, whatever I want, cost is no object."

Ava called over from the card table, "Tell the truth, Irving. Tell my sister you eat with the chauffeur, not with your daughter. When does *she* come? The last time was when you fell out of the elevator and broke your elbow."

"Never mind. The chauffeur is like a son to me," Irving called back. "Better than a son. Don't lose your concentration, Ava—those cardsharps over there will cheat you blind if they get one chance."

"I'm ahead four dollars, already, Irving," Ava informed him, ". . . and the night is young." Each time, she pronounced his name "Oiving," and Anna winced. The Bronx still lived in full color in Ava—nothing could winnow it out. The Bronx sat on Ava's tongue like a wart. Anna herself was certain she had no trace of any crude accent. She tried to speak like an American descended from someone who came over on the Mayflower.

"Listen to this one," Irving said. "Two old men are playing golf, but their eyes are so bad they can't see where the ball lands. A third *alta cocka* comes by and says he has
154 perfect eyesight, he'll help them out. He'll watch the ball for them. So one of them hits the ball and then asks, 'So did you see where it landed?' The *alta cocka* says, 'Of course I saw, I got perfect eyesight.' 'So where is it?' the golfer says. 'I forgot,' says the old man."

"An Alzheimer joke! For shame!" Sadie said. "With Ida sitting right here and poor Herman upstairs, putting on his socks backwards this minute."

Irving's attention was drawn away as a fire truck and an ambulance raced by, their sirens screaming. "What's your hurry?" Irving asked, waving his hand at them in dismissal.

Anna's eyes had adjusted to the darkness, and she watched Irving's bald head wobbling on his turkey neck. His ears were huge; they hung on his skull like some strange invention. Certain animals, when she saw them on nature programs, made her feel this way. They adapted to their environment without regard for polite shapes. She didn't want to have to look at their hanging pouches or spiky chins or poison sacs. Old people, too, grew strange parts, took on camouflaging skin pigments, adopted peculiar postures and gaits. Anna hated belonging to an indelicate species.

"Another cowboy bites the dust," Irving said as the tail-lights of the ambulance disappeared. "Who knows who'll be next?"

"Comes an earthquake we'll all be gone," Anna pronounced.

"Here we have hurricanes," Irving told her. "At least get your catastrophes straight."

"A flush!" Ava said with a cry of glee, laying down her cards. She swept the pile of coins in the kitty toward her.

"Believe me, you can't take it with you," Irving predicted. "Slow down, Ava, enjoy the sights."

"I'm done, anyway . . . it's time for us to go up," Ava said. "*Wheel of Fortune* is on in five minutes." The four ladies pushed back their chairs and stood up. Ava tapped the cards into a neat little square and set the deck down on the table. She gathered up her big pile of quarters and dropped them in the jacket of her flowered pantsuit. She **155** adjusted her mink.

"You ladies live by the game shows," Irving said. "But look, right here, isn't life the biggest game show of all?"

"You're giving away trips to Hawaii?" Sadie asked him. "If you're giving away free cruises, we'll stay and watch you."

"I told you before, Sadie—you want a cruise, I'll take you on a cruise."

"When I'm that desperate, I'll let you know."

"I'm going upstairs now, Anna," Ava said. "Come with me."

"Maybe I'll stay here a while. I could do without the *Wheel of Fortune*," Anna said.

Ava shot her a look, the same kind of look she'd sent her when Anna had been flower girl at Ava's wedding in 1914 and stepped on her train, causing Ava to stumble. "Come up," Ava demanded. "Irving sits here all night. Irving is always here. You'll see him when we come down again from nine to ten to watch the sideshow going by," Ava assured her.

"Your sister thinks this is the army, she lives by a schedule," Irving mumbled into the dark. Anna had noticed this was true: Ava woke at eight, ate toast dipped in coffee poured into her saucer, watched the *$25,000 Pyramid*, watched *Cardsharks*, watched the daytime *Wheel of For-*

tune, came down for poker till Meals on Wheels arrived, ate lunch from Styrofoam boxes with the other ladies on the porch (a drumstick, yellow wax beans, a slice of white bread, a cup of bouillon soup and some Jell-O). After lunch, a nap, then an *I Love Lucy* rerun, then down to the porch for card playing till dinnertime, then up for dinner, then down again for cards, then up again for TV, then down again for one last blast of bus fumes on the porch. On certain days there were doctor appointments, and once a week the trip in Hyman Cohen's hotel station wagon to the Food Circus.

156   As Anna walked by Irving's big feet to follow Ava into the lobby, he reached out for her hand. He had the nerve to grab it and squeeze it for a couple of seconds before he let it go. She looked down into his blue eyes and saw him smiling up at her. "Laugh a little, sweetheart," he said. "There's no good jokes six feet under."

A strange sensation woke Anna; the room glowed blue with particles of light reflected from the shimmering signs of the Crown and the Cadillac. No air came in the lowered windows. Ava never ran the air conditioner: she said it was too noisy, but Anna knew it was the expense. Ava had always been a miser. When they had talked long distance, arranging the visit, Ava had promised Anna a room of her own "right across the hall from mine, one with its own TV," but when Anna had arrived at the Colby Plaza, the first thing Ava said was, "I got a cot in my room for you so you wouldn't have to be all alone. It worried me, you should be all alone in a strange place."

The cot is cheaper, Anna thought, but then was sorry to think badly of her sister who was soon, no doubt, to depart this vale of tears. Ava lay only a foot away breathing noisily through her open mouth. The segments of her false teeth shone like some plastic toy. The room made Anna feel claustrophobic: two beds, a stove, a sink, a refrigerator, a dining table, a dresser, a TV, a recliner chair. All Ava's worldly goods were here; from her huge, human life—a husband, children, big decisions to make—to this: *Wheel of Fortune*, Meals on Wheels, poker, little tiny portions of milk frozen in margarine containers to last the week. (Anna already lived this way in LA; it wasn't news to her but to see that her powerful sister had come to this was a shock.)

She tried to go back to sleep. She kept remembering how Irving had grabbed her hand. An old turkey. A no one. Still, his fingers had felt alive. There was heat and strength in them. She had felt something, a feeling. This was astonishing, to feel something and to think about it. To bother to think about something and to feel pleasure from it.

157

Anna tiptoed out of bed, put on her clothes, and went down in the old elevator to the lobby. The light of dawn was just arriving through the windows; the desk clerk, a Cuban named Jesús who always wore a dirty black suit, was sleeping on one of the old couches. Anna didn't know what to do with herself. The cards from last night, she saw, were still on the table outside. She could play solitaire. She could actually walk to the ocean and watch the sunrise.

Would it be dangerous? To go alone to the beach? Did they have muggers in Miami Beach? Never mind muggers, she would go anyway. At her age forget everything. Doom was just as likely hiding in her arteries as on the sand.

Irving was still outside on the front porch, sleeping in his chair, his head back against the stucco wall. Had he really been there all night? Anna stared. She thought she could see dew condensed on his bald head. His white shoes glowed in the dimness. Maybe he was dead. She went over to him and tapped on his skull. He jerked upright.

"Dummy," she said with relief. "You don't have a bed?"

"I wasn't sleeping," he said, straightening his eye glasses. "Just taking the air."

"Who cares?" Anna said. "I'm going beachcombing."

"I'll come with you."

"I'm going alone," Anna said. "I need an adventure. When did I ever see the sunrise? In California, you only get sunsets. And at the end of the day, who's going to run to the beach?"

"Here no one runs, we all walk," Irving explained, as he creaked himself out of the chair. He offered Anna his arm. "But allow me to come along and be your bodyguard."

They saw it happen, a fuzz of pink over the blue horizon, a blur of white cloud, and then the emerging burning ball, coming up on a fountain of flame.

158   "That alone," Irving said, standing against the rail of the narrow, boardwalk while seagulls screeched and wheeled overhead, ". . . and you could believe in God."

"You believe?" Anna asked.

"What am I, some kind of sucker?"

"Smart people, really smart people—some of them are believers."

"I'll take my medicine straight," Irving said. "I'll face the firing squad without a blindfold."

"It would be nice to believe something," Anna said. "Then you could have reasons, you could have meaning, you could have a social center, you could have someone to say a prayer when you're dead. This way, like for my husband Abram, I had to hire a stranger, a baby calling himself a rabbi, he reads from a printed sheet 'This was a good man, a good husband, a good father.' A know-nothing."

"If I were going to believe, I'd choose Jesus," Irving said. "He's the best deal around. But no one in Miami Beach, Florida, in the Jew-nited States of America, thinks he's worth two cents."

"They prefer Moses?"

"He can't hold a candle. All he did was talk to God in the burning bush. The trouble is, when you're this old, you should have something to hang on to."

"How old?"

"Ninety-two," Irving said. "Come June."

"My husband died at fifty-five," Anna said. "You had a whole lifetime extra over him."

"It's never enough," Irving said. "It doesn't feel like I even started yet."

They began to walk along the wooden boardwalk. Two seagulls lit on the railing and walked right up to them. They stared boldly, craning their beaks forward.

"They want something," Anna said.

"So who doesn't?" Irving answered. The sun was well out of the ocean now, getting redder.

159

"Look," Anna said. "Is that beautiful or is that beautiful?"

"You're what's beautiful," Irving said.

"Don't get carried away, Irving," Anna said. "My week is up. I'm going home tomorrow, and anyway I'm not available."

"My mistake. The first day I saw you on the porch we should have got acquainted. I should have talked to you sooner. You got a boyfriend?"

"My heart belongs to Arthur Rubinstein," Anna said.

"He's younger than me? Richer?"

"Never mind," Anna said. "It's not going anywhere with Arthur and me."

"Even at our age we have a right to pleasure," Irving said.

"Don't lump yourself together with me," Anna said. "You're old enough to be my father. Look how you can hardly walk and I'm limber on my toes like a ballet dancer."

"It's these rubber soles," he explained. "New shoes. They glue me down. It's like wearing suction cups."

"You want to go on the sand?" Anna asked. "You want to stick your toes in the water?"

"In my heart, I'm running down to the waves already,"

Irving said, stopping to lean on the rail, breathing hard. "I'm splashing you with water. I'm ducking you under."

"And I'm jumping over waves," Anna said, looking out at the blue wide ocean.

"I'm tickling you," Irving said.

"I'm laughing," Anna said. She turned her head away from him.

"So how come you're crying?" Irving asked after a minute.

"Because it's a pity," Anna said, wiping her eyes with a tissue. "What we used to have, and what we can't have anymore."

160

"At least let's take what we can get," Irving said. He held out his hand. Anna studied it. Then she crooked her fingers in his. He brought their hands up to his mouth and kissed Anna's fingers. "I'm doing more than this with you," he said. "Much more. You understand what I mean?"

"Don't have a dirty mind," Anna said.

"I'm doing everything," Irving said. "Every sweet thing. We're in heaven."

Anna was silent.

"I'm going too far?" Irving asked.

"No," Anna said. "I appreciate it."

The next afternoon, the last of her visit, when the Red Top Cab had been called and was to pick her up in one hour for the trip to the airport, Anna put on her new silky flowered dress and got everything else into her suitcase. Ava was already down on the front porch playing cards. Anna realized that if she stayed here for a year, the sister business wouldn't improve. Ava wasn't going to get sentimental. A big bossy sister stays a big bossy sister. To cheer herself up, she sprayed herself five times with Ava's expensive perfume, and by the time she rode down in the elevator with her suitcase she smelled like a lilac tree. She would be lucky if in two minutes there weren't bees landing all over her head.

Irving was spiffy in a plaid jacket and a red bow tie.

He saluted her from his chair. "Forgive me if even on this farewell occasion I don't stand up," he said. "One knee isn't so good today."

"Stand up anyway, Irving," Ava called over to him. "Use it or you'll lose it."

"He lost it already," Sadie said, with a hoarse laugh. "Otherwise I'd go with him on a cruise."

"I didn't lose it, sweetheart," he said, getting red in the face. "I just don't give it away to big-mouth yentas." He turned to Anna. "You're lucky you're getting out of here. If I could go with you, I'd run in a minute."

161

"So where am I going that's so special?" Anna said, suddenly seeing a picture in her mind of her tiny dark apartment, of her pianos, two of them, with the lids down over the keys, of the milk going sour in the refrigerator.

"Maybe you could get a room here," Irving suggested. "You know," he called over to the ladies at the card table, "I don't think Hyman rented the room yet from after when Sam Kriskin died."

"No thank you," Anna said. "I'm not interested in living in a dead man's room."

"He didn't die in the room," Irving assured her. "Only on the way in the ambulance. Not a single bad thing happened in the room. Kriskin was an immaculate person. That man was as clean as holy water."

"What's the rent?" Anna said. It was a question she didn't expect to ask. It was meaningless, it was to make talk. It was stupid to have brought it up, what did she care? In LA she had a very good rent-controlled apartment, and, besides, she would never leave her daughters, what for? To come here and sit with some old man?

But Irving's blue eyes shone like electrified marbles, and he was already getting up slowly from the red metal chair. "We'll go in the lobby, Anna," he said. "We'll find out the rent, maybe you'll stay, then what a time we'll have, you

and I—we'll go across to the Crown every night and watch
the floor show, we'll go out to dinner on Sundays with my
daughter's chauffeur, we'll buy a VCR and rent a
movie . . ."

Irving started to walk without his feet. Anna saw his
upper body move toward her, but his shoes, his white shoes
with the red rubber soles, stayed glued to the cement and
she saw him go down like a boulder.

When she opened her eyes the next instant, he was face
down on the cement porch and no one even noticed it. Ava
was dealing a new hand of cards.

162   Irving, rolling on his round belly, was silent. He turned
his head slightly to the side, and Anna saw his cracked eye
glasses and blood on his forehead.

"Oh God," she cried out. "Look over here!"

Irving whimpered a little and stayed on his face.

"Oh—help me pick him up, *please!*" Anna cried. She
could not bend down alone because of her osteoporosis and
her arthritis and her collapsed vertebrae.

"We don't pick anyone up here," Sadie said from the
table. "We each got our own problems. In no time flat we
could all land in the hospital."

"They fall here every day," Ida added.

"How many times has Irving fallen anyway?" Mickey
asked, and all the women looked skyward, as if they were
figuring.

Anna couldn't bear it, to see him gasping and jerking like
a beached fish down there, his forehead on cement. She
rushed into the lobby and grabbed a cushion from one of
the sagging couches. She carried it outside and slid it under
Irving's forehead.

"Don't move him," Ava said. "Something could be broken."

"The last time nothing was broken," Ida said.

"But the time before, remember, it was his elbow."

"This was a softer fall than that one. That time, he

stepped out the elevator before it was level. Everyone heard him go down."

Anna ran inside again and yelled to the Cuban clerk. "Jesús! Call the doctor, dummy!" He seemed to be counting out colored postcards of the Colby Plaza. He was counting in Spanish.

Outside again, Anna knelt over Irving. "Irving, can you hear me?" He rocked on his round stomach to answer her. "Are you okay, Irving?" she asked him. "Are you comfortable?"

"I make a nice living," he said.

Anna looked at him, then stood up, shocked.   **163**

"A joke," he said. Then he spit out a little blood.

"Jesús!" she yelled into the lobby "Did you call?" The man looked up from the desk, puzzled. It occurred to Anna that he was drunk.

"Hey," he said suddenly. "That old guy can't be on that pillow." He ran out to the porch and grabbed the cushion from under Irving's forehead. "If he bleeds on this, Hyman Cohen will blow a fit! These are his new pillows!"

"Ten years new," Ava called over to them.

"Jesús! Come here!" She called him like a dog, slapping her leg. "Help me pick him up this minute!"

"There's no hurry," the Cuban said. "They'll pick him up when they come."

"Who?"

"The paramedics."

"Did you call them?"

"They have a standing appointment here," Sadie said from the card table as she lit another cigarette.

"Go," Anna said, shoving the Cuban. "Call them!" She watched him till he went in and picked up the phone.

While they waited, Anna sat down on the steps of the Colby Plaza and maneuvered Irving's face, still pointing down, into her lap. She stroked the few hairs on the back of his bald head.

"Don't worry, Irving darling," she whispered. "You'll be fine, this is just a little nothing. We all have days like this. I myself fell in a hole in a parking lot a year ago. I still have a bone spur on my foot from it."

Irving was crying.

"It hurts you somewhere? It hurts a lot?"

He nodded his head. His weight in her lap felt like the weight of one of her babies. She thought the feeling of taking care had disappeared forever, and now here it was again.

"Here they come," Ava announced.

164   A shuddering vibration shook the street, and a fire truck pulled up at the curb. Four firemen jumped off; they were wearing black rubber trousers with yellow suspenders.

"Aah, it's you again, isn't it?" one of them said to Irving. Irving was sobbing without restraint now. She could feel his hot tears seep through her dress. She found his hand and squeezed it. He held on very tight.

"Don't worry, Irving dear," she whispered into his ear. "It's only this life-and-death business we're having here. Don't take it seriously."

The firemen were turning him over, opening a big black box, taking out rubber tubes, gauze, fancy machines. If the firemen were being the doctors, then were the doctors running up and down ladders putting out fires?

The paramedics clumped around in their huge rubber boots. "Anything hurt?" they kept asking Irving. "Where does it hurt?"

"He's fine," Ava called from the card table. "The man is made of steel. I warned him, never wear shoes with rubber soles. And I told him, always get up slow, get your balance first. But no, a big shot, he was in a hurry to impress my sister."

Anna shot her a look, like the look Ava had shot Anna in 1914.

"Here comes the ambulance," one of the firemen said.

"Are you going to the hospital with him?" He was addressing Anna.

"Yes," Anna said, and at the same instant Ava called out,
"No, of course she isn't going. Let his daughter go."

"My daughter never comes," Irving cried, crushing
Anna's hand now that he was sitting up, propped by the
firemen.

"I'll come with you," Anna said. "Don't worry,"

"Don't be a fool," Ava said. She was finally talking directly to Anna, paying her the attention that she hadn't
given in the whole visit, pulling her up by the arm. "You'll
have to wait there seven hours. That's how long they make
you wait in Emergency. It's stacked to the ceiling with old
people who fell down." 165

"I have time," Anna said.

"No you don't," Ava said. "The cab is here,"

Anna had forgotten entirely. The Red Top. The airport.
The plane. LA. Her pianos with the shrouded keys.

"Take her suitcase," Ava instructed the driver who had
come up onto the porch and was staring, open-mouthed, at
Irving. Ava pushed Anna toward the steps. Her mink's
head, slithering on her shoulder, showed its tiny razor-
sharp teeth.

"Take her to the airport," Ava instructed the cab driver.
"And you . . .," she said to the ambulance driver, "you get
going and take *him* to the hospital."

Irving reached out to Anna, and Anna reached for Irving. But the forces were too strong, the time was too late.
They were too powerless. Two minutes later they were rushing in opposite directions—she could feel the wind tearing
them apart, the seagulls were going every which way over
the ocean—and Anna couldn't tell if the sirens she heard
were approaching or receding.

STARRY NIGHT

Looking out the window of the bus, Anna could see a pandemonium of gold and glitter—the whole world rushing around crazily, buying presents. On Wilshire Boulevard, people were stabbing each other with the sharp edges of their packages. Christmas season was a mean season—fat Santa Clauses ringing their bells in everyone's faces, carols blasting out of loudspeakers, "Let-Us-Adore-Him" and "Christ-the-Lord" in every song. Christmas was a terrible imposition on the Jews. Anna, who had no use for rituals, had made it a special point all her life to ignore Christmas. She left the radio off, didn't venture out, read only the newspaper's front page, which had no ads. Long ago she had told her children, "No presents for me. All I want from you is that you should be happy." Her youngest daughter was a suicide's widow and had health problems; her oldest girl had money troubles. The truth was she should have allowed them to give her store-bought presents. With her fancy rules, they could give her nothing.

Now, two days away from Christmas, she was on her way to the doctor's. All the old people on the bus seemed lame or asthmatic; they were probably all going to the doctor's, and, like her, they were going alone. What could she expect from a world in which a woman of seventy-eight had to take three buses by herself to visit a doctor? At least, in the old days, doctors had made house calls.

An old man was making his way up the aisle, stopping

beside each seat. He swayed beside Anna as if he might land in her lap. He was unshaven and wearing a tattered coat. Thrusting his fist under Anna's nose, he offered her a choice of red-striped candy canes. She turned her head sharply, dismissing him. He had probably put cyanide in them. He bent closer, shaking the cellophane bouquet beside her ear until she locked eyes with him and willed him away.

Well, soon she would be done with Christmases and all the rest of it. How long? She couldn't guess. The years no longer had any definition—one year was like the snap of a finger, no time at all, a mere one seventy-eighth of her life, almost too small a space to count. When she had first learned to play the piano, at seven, a year had been one seventh of her life. To get from her dull Hanon exercises to her first Chopin nocturne had been an eternity of scales, chords, harmony exercises; endless afternoons of winding her metronome and letting its upright brass ticker measure out the practice hours, the beats, the notes that carried her like tiny black birds, away from the raucous life on the lower east side of New York, and later from the wastes of Brooklyn.

Now Anna had trouble with her eyes: the birds waiting on the staff, as if poised on telephone wires, were bunched erratically, blurred together, bumping one another as they waited for her signal. She had trouble with her fingers, too: when the birds began to fly they became lost in black, dense clouds, their delicate shapes concealed, their formations blotted. Her trills, once absolute bells of clarity, sounded now like the rumble of the "el" thundering by when she was a little girl.

A tremendous blast caused Anna to jump halfway out of her seat. A black boy carrying a radio as big as a house had just turned up the volume, and "Silent Night" was coming at her like the open palm of her father's hand. Automatically she pressed her lips together and held her breath.

168

Her father was dead sixty years and he could still do this to her! Though he had been out of Poland eight years when she entered the public schools of New York, he had stubbornly forbidden her to sing Christmas carols with the other children. She was allowed only to move her lips during the school's Christmas performances on such phrases as "round yon virgin" and "holy infant." He had instructed her, fiercely, with his hand held up and ready to smack, to weld her lips shut, to be certain that not a flicker of her breath passed through her vocal cords when the forbidden phrase "Christ the Lord" came up. He had been like a madman on the subject, though in most other ways he was a kind and reasonable man.

169

Anna noticed suddenly that all the old people on the bus were now sucking on red candy canes. They looked like a gathering of lunatics. All of them on their way to their doctors, or to nowhere. Being alive was such a commotion and took so much effort. Why shouldn't they suck on something sweet? What better was there to do?

"So I have a joke for you, Mrs. Goldman," said Dr. Rifkin, her eye doctor, as soon as he walked into the examining room. Silver tinsel hung from the rubber plant against the wall, and the doctor had a little red-and-green Christmas wreath pinned to his white coat. "Four *Yiddishe* mamas get together to play cards." He motioned Anna into the chair where he would tell her how fast she was going blind. He was tall, homely, and overweight. If her daughters had married doctors, they wouldn't be having health problems and money problems.

"The first lady says, '*Oy.*' The second one says, '*Oy vey.*' The third one says, '*Oy vey is mir.*' The fourth one says, "*Ladies, ladies! We promised we wouldn't talk about our children!*' "

Dr. Rifkin laughed loudly at his joke and motioned for Anna to put her chin in the cup. Anna flinched at his deep laughter. She wasn't in that class of women, she resented being thought of as a *Yiddishe* mama and she never played cards.

"So how is life treating you, Mrs. Goldman?" the doctor asked, turning wheels on his machine.

"I don't see well and my fingers don't move where I want them to when I play my Mozart sonatas," she said pointedly.

"Then you're extra lucky to be Jewish. You know why?" he asked, holding the eye dropper right over her head. "You can always play on the keys with your nose!"

Anna frowned, letting the numbing drops freeze the surface of her eyes. He darkened the room, and a burning blue light materialized in front of Anna's face. She stared into the heart of it, feeling it burn into her mind. The doctor's head loomed an inch away. Not since Abram's death, except for these visits to Dr. Rifkin, had she felt a man's breath or heard his heavy breathing. When the measurements were taken and the lights turned on—with the doctor again a safe distance away—she steadied herself. It was her opportunity to introduce a new subject.

"Doctor—how often do you think my daughters should have their eyes examined now that I have this condition?" Anna could never ask doctors enough questions, and they never gave her satisfactory answers.

"Oh—once every year or so."

"Not more often?"

"If they want to go more often—sure."

"Shouldn't they go every six months, so if this same problem turns up due to bad heredity, they won't go blind?"

"Mrs. Goldman," said Dr. Rifkin, "what's the difference between a Jewish mother and a vulture?"

"I have no idea," Anna said coldly.

"A vulture only eats hearts after they're dead. A Jewish mother eats her heart out all her life."

• • •

The Christmas tree in the waiting room was broken out in
an epidemic of angels; around its fake moss base, empty
gift-wrapped boxes were piled. A curly-haired little boy of
about four shook each box and then sadly set it down. Anna
sat across the room from his parents with her heart pounding. She was to have laser surgery in half an hour. "Your
intraocular pressure is way up," Dr. Rifkin had told her.
"Not much point in depending on the drops any longer. I'd
usually schedule you for another day, but I'm going away
for a couple of weeks and we should nip this in the bud. If
you can wait till I'm done with my next patient, I'll tell Sally
to get things ready, and we'll get this over with. It doesn't
hurt, it doesn't take long, you shouldn't have much pain
afterward, just a little irritation."

"How do you do it?" Anna had asked. "I've heard it's
done without knives, without anesthesia."

"You want me to tell you everything I learned in medical
school in two minutes?"

"I just want to know something about what to expect."

"It's magic," said Dr. Rifkin, patting her rudely on the
arm. "Don't worry about it. Don't you think I know my
stuff?"

The receptionist had asked Anna to sign a release, so if
she died it was no one's fault. The procedure was going to
cost a thousand dollars. No wonder the doctor could tell
jokes all day. She hoped Medicare would pay some of it. In
a few minutes she would be taking part in a magic trick. A
vulture would be pulled from her heart, pluck out her eyes,
and replace in their sockets two cold blue marbles. A man
in a black cape would saw her body in half.

"Do you have a candy cane for me?" the little boy said,
coming to Anna and putting his hand on her knee.

"Donny, come back here and don't bother the lady. Not
everyone gives out candy canes."

"It's okay," Anna said, regretting her suspicions on the
bus. "I have grandchildren. I wish I had a candy cane to

171

give him. He's a sweet boy." Anna wondered what was wrong with him; glued in the middle of his forehead, like a great eye, was a silver snap. The boy touched it.

"Don't wrinkle the lady's skirt. Behave yourself," the boy's mother said. His father added, "Don't touch your electrode." The parents were young, and looked terrified. She knew they weren't from Beverly Hills. Anna didn't dare ask them what she wanted to know. *Is your boy going blind? Does he have a brain tumor? Something worse?* The boy had climbed on the couch beside Anna and wiggled his bottom against the backrest. His hand on her thigh was warm through her skirt. The boy's mother, sitting across the room with the father, said apologetically, "He probably thinks you're going to read to him. His grandmother always reads to him. You look a little like her . . . my mother."

Anna felt the boy's warmth all down her side. His head brushed against her arm. She could smell his talcum powder, which reminded her of her own sweet babies, of that vanished other life. "I have nothing to read to him, but I can draw him a picture."

"Oh, he'd love that. Donny, come here and give the nice lady your colored pencils. She'll draw a picture for you."

The boy scrambled off the couch and ran across the room for the little flat box of pencils and a pad of paper. "I always come prepared," the mother explained. "We have to wait for hours sometimes."

"Where are you from?" Anna asked.

"Nevada."

"That's a long way," Anna acknowledged.

"We don't mind coming far," the father said. "We would go farther. We would go anywhere."

"Wherever the experts are," the mother explained.

"Well, Donny—I only know how to draw one picture." Anna said. "I'm a one-picture artist. I used to draw a picture for my little girls. Shall I draw it for you?"

The child nodded his head energetically. The electrode

172

mirrored the artificial candles flashing on the tree and sent
bursts of red light into Anna's sensitive eyes. She took the
boy's warm little hand and held onto it for a minute.

"Well, now, here we go."

On the tablet she drew in pink the heart-shaped face of a
girl. "Let's call her Wendy," Anna said. With the yellow
pencil, she gave Wendy tight corkscrew curls and wavy
bangs. Her eyelashes, done in black feathery strokes, were
long and demure. Her mouth was a little strawberry rose-
bud.

"What is Wendy doing?" the child asked, looking up at
Anna as she drew little red x's to the edge of the paper.   173

"She's giving you a hundred kisses," Anna said. "Like
this." She lowered her head and kissed the boy on his
forehead, next to the silver circle. "She wants to be your
sweetheart."

"Thank you," the boy's mother said. "Thank you very
much."

From down the hall, someone called Donny's name.

"Here we go, Donny boy," his father said. Both parents
stood. The father hoisted the boy to his hip.

"Good luck," Anna said. "I wish you all the luck in the
world."

Anna still had the pad and pencils in her lap. She began
to draw a house. It was a child's version of a house, one-
dimensional, with a door and two windows, and a chimney
on the roof which had a spiral of smoke spilling from it into
the sky. Inside was a happy family. She drew the sun and
birds flying. She made the birds into little black notes and
drew telephone wires for them to perch on.

Then, as if by magic, Anna saw the pastel chalk drawing
of a cottage in the country materialize before her eyes. At
the edge of the cottage a stream flowed by under a
weathered wooden bridge. The season was fall, and the
leaves lay in brilliant shifting hills along the road. Dr.

Pincus from Brooklyn was drawing the picture, sitting on
the edge of the bed of Anna's oldest girl, Janet. He had just
told them Janet had pneumonia again. The snowflakes
which had fallen from his coat were melting on the rug at
his feet. Janet had already had her painful injection and
lay limp, tears on her cheeks; every December since she had
started school she had been too sick to attend or take part
in the Christmas play. On this day she seemed to take little
comfort from the doctor's reassuring voice telling her that
her fever would fall, her chest would stop hurting, her
cough would subside. Dr. Pincus had looked around the
room and asked Anna if she wouldn't mind bringing to the
bedside Janet's blackboard, mounted on a rickety easel.
The doctor had stayed there with Janet for a long time,
sitting on the edge of her bed, drawing the landscape very
carefully in pastel chalks: a woodfire sending smoke from
the chimney, a chipmunk on a fencepost, a high and distant
formation of geese honking across the sky. When last of all
he had drawn a graceful young girl with swinging braids—
unmistakably Janet—skipping rope on the wooden bridge,
Janet had laughed weakly, and Dr. Pincus had said, "That's
my girl. That's what I've been waiting to hear."

Janet, that winter, had again missed being in the Christmas play at school, but she had healed. She had lived to
grow up and have money troubles. It was Dr. Pincus who
had urged Anna and Abram to move with their children out
of the bitter winters of New York. Twenty years ago Abram
had died in California of leukemia. Doctor Pincus was
surely dead by now. Doctors had stopped making house
calls, and Anna was about to have her eyes pierced by laser
beams.

"Here's a joke for you," Dr. Rifkin said in the operating
room. "A middle-aged woman comes home from the doctor
and says to her husband, 'The doctor tells me I have
breasts like a twenty-five year old.' The husband answers,

174

'And what did he say about your fifty-year old ass?' 'Oh,'
says the wife, 'he didn't mention you at all!' ' "

Dr. Rifkin guffawed. Anna sat like a block of ice while the
nurse strapped her head into a contraption.

"Hold your head very still now," the doctor said. "Here
we go."

Meteors flew into Anna's old eyes, deep into her brain,
where she felt her precious memories hiding their faces.
Again and again the doctor fired flaming star showers at
her, in the shapes of her husband and children holding out
their arms to her, and in the forms of quarter notes, eighth
notes, sixteenth notes. She waited for a whole note to come   **175**
flying to her.

"That's it, Mrs. Goldman," the doctor said. "Go home
and no jumping rope this afternoon. Come back in one
week. No—make it two, I'll be in Hawaii. Happy holidays,
and don't worry. Worry never did anyone any good and
never changed the outcome of anything."

"You don't have to tell *me*," Anna said.

When Anna got home, she fell back on her bed in gratitude and relief that she was alive and still had her vision.
She turned on the television on her nighttable and saw a
great throng of people looking heavenward, their mouths
wide open, like baby birds about to receive nourishment.
The conductor was on a high podium; the young and the old
in the great auditorium had open songbooks in their hands.
Their faces were aglow as they sang:

> *For unto us a Child is born,*
> *Unto us a Son is given . . .*

The words flashed across the screen as they sang; the eyes
of the singers sparkled with light while the camera moved
slowly from face to face. Anna was about to switch channels—what did she need this Christmas junk for?—when

the camera stopped and held fast upon the face of a very old woman. She was older than Anna, her features no longer unique, but sunken into a mask of great age. Yet her mouth quivered with passionate energy, and her eyes reflected light as bright as laser beams. Anna sank back on her pillows and attended with half her mind until she heard the soprano sing some words about "the Saviour, which is Christ the Lord."

She stiffened—the same old thing. Anna could feel her father's angry gaze upon her: *Turn that off! Hold your breath. Move only your lips. Don't sing! Clasp your mouth shut! Never say those words!* With an exasperated flap of her hand, Anna held her father off. She felt a flare of fury blaze up in her. She was only interested in the music, didn't he know that? He had bought her her first piano. He had taken her to hear Caruso sing at the Metropolitan Opera house. He, of all people, should know that music was music, and nothing was going to change her at this point in her life.

176

What fascinated Anna was the evidence of pure happiness which shone on the faces of the singers. There wasn't a mean streak showing anywhere. The camera presented her with an intimate, almost embarrassing, close-up view. She could see pock marks on some faces, little beauty marks and dimples on others. She was much closer than she ever could have been in person—only an inch away from a fat woman; squeezed in with a crowd of young people wearing sweatshirts adorned with the words "Sing Along Messiah"; almost touching a handsome bearded man who looked like Christ Himself. She was right there beside a pregnant woman, brushing arms with a father bending over to point out to his son the correct place in the score—she was with husbands and wives and children, and they were all as happy as Anna had ever seen anyone in her life. The conductor waving his wand was happy. The violinists in the orchestra were smiling as they played, the trumpets shot rainbows of light into the air, the harpsichord strings vi-

brated and caused a shimmering high above in the great
vaulted ceiling of the hall. The soprano sang:

Rejoice greatly, O daughter of Zion . . .

Anna, a Jew, was definitely a daughter of Zion. If *she*
wasn't, who was? It was too late to discuss this with her
father. Anna had lived a long time, and all her life, without
question, she had turned her eyes away from the steeples of
churches, away from paintings of Jesus in museums, away
from gold crosses on the necks of men and women in the
street. Anna's eyes burned as she studied the rapt singers.   177
She listened, unthreatened, with the ears of her natural
skepticism:

Then shall the eyes of the blind be opened, and the ears of
the deaf unstopped, then shall the lame man leap as an
hart, and the tongue of the dumb shall sing.

Suddenly slapping her bed with the palm of her hand,
Anna addressed her father: *Papa, listen to the music!*
Something was causing happiness to shine on those faces.
Something made that old man on the bus give out his candy
canes, made Dr. Rifkin, for all his joking, sit there behind
his magic machine-gun to do what he could do to keep Anna
seeing the world. Someone had invented that one-eyed silver electrode to shine in the middle of Donny's forehead.
    Anna felt, without doubt, that every one of the singers
was beautiful. It was not like her, it was not her way.
Normally she would have made private notations to herself
about this one's fake blonde hair with dark roots showing,
or that one's bad skin, or the morals of the careless young
that the world turned out these days—those braless sloppy
girls and the boys with green hair and gold studs in their
ears. Old women with scarves around their turkey-skin
necks could never fool her. She always had ready, in neat

bars of music, a song of many ungenerous verses waiting to be sung. But the music in her head had modulated. She wondered if the surgery had changed her vision in some profound way. She felt like putting her arms around each person in the singing throng—the scarred, the fat, the heavily made-up, the too pretty to be true. When the chorus sang:

Surely he hath borne our griefs . . .

Anna thought she would buy her daughters presents. Maybe she would ask them to buy *her* a present. What did she want? A record of Handel's *Messiah*? Her father had his hand up, ready to hit. *Leave me alone!* she told him. *So what if I don't hold my breath when those words come around! You've made a big mistake. You worry too much.*

She felt funny, a little like laughing. A little like singing. She wasn't much of a laugher or a singer. She hadn't sung in perhaps seventy years. But she lived alone in a little apartment—who was going to judge her? Sitting up straight in her bed, she smoothed back her hair as if she were about to take her place in the crowd and be shown on television, her eyes twinkling with light. Nervously, she began to sing along as the words appeared on the screen. It took a while for her to get used to the sound of her own thin, wavering voice rising in her darkened bedroom, but soon she gained volume and strength, and finally, with confidence, she brought herself in tune with the others.

178

TICKETS TO
DONAHUE
. . . .

A truck driver with an extremely important mustache
(also with muscles like braids poking out the sleeves of his T-
shirt) stared straight at Anna, dared her with his eyes to
keep staring at him. He sat high in his shiny red rig and, for
an instant, when he turned his head around to reach for a
cigarette, she could see the points of his mustache sticking
out from behind his ears. He'd parked his truck directly in
front of the NBC Studios on Alameda Street, leaving it
there to belch diesel fumes into Anna and Gert's faces while
they stood on line for the *Donahue* show. He showed no
signs of moving on. Anna knew his breed—the kind of man
who tried to stare you down, who thought if he tried long
enough he could get you to think the way he was thinking.
She'd worked on Wall Street in the thirties and had enough
of those stares from men on subway platforms who were
forever trying to get a look at her ankles.

Anna noticed with satisfaction that Gert was watching the
way the truckdriver was staring at her. Men had always
been after Anna (her ankles were still elegant), and Gert
had always been shocked. Gert didn't understand the
power of sex. To this day she bragged about having been a
virgin at thirty-nine when she married the first of her two
old husbands. A sister so backward was an embarrassment
to Anna. Barney had bowled Gert over with a few bouquets
of wilted flowers stolen from a neighbor's garden. Anna had
tried to set Gert straight; she had known at once Barney

was an opportunist, a taker. He had children he was going to look out for first—all he wanted from Gert was someone to cook his dinners and iron his shirts. Anna understood human nature, but Gert was willing to be fooled. She had prayed for a trousseau all her life, and for one red lace nightgown she was willing to take on a man who, as part of the agreement, insisted on dragging his teenaged daughter to live with them. This was a girl who slept, snoring, on a cot in the living room. This was a girl who ate sardines with her fingers. Even when Gert learned (from Anna, who had done plenty of detective work) that Barney was giving most **180** of his company's profits to his sons and crying poor to Gert, Gert was willing to forgive him. The sons had families, she explained to Anna—they *needed* more.

That was the kind of fool she was. Anna wondered how she and Gert had ever come to be sisters, born in the same family, from the same mother and father, in the same house, only two years apart. Even now—as the two of them stood reflected in the truck's gleaming side—their resemblance ended with their white hair. Gert was dolled up in a ruffled pink-flowered dress and wearing a necklace of arthritic coral sticks, which were jabbing her neck, while Anna wore a simple tailored beige blouse and brown skirt. Gert liked to wear a lot of makeup, and Anna wore none. They looked accidentally thrown together: a hillbilly and a woman from a list of the year's Ten Best Dressed. Anna noticed her frown reflected in the truck's side and immediately let her face relax. Their mother used to threaten them with dire results: one day their ugly expressions would freeze that way forever. Gert had always taken the warning seriously— she kept a cow-like smile on her face. If she saw babies, old ladies, dogs in the street, she'd greet them with soft, sympa- thetic cow eyes. She'd never figured out that babies grew up to be like anyone else who robbed you, but a person couldn't explain such things to Gert. Gert was the original Pollyanna.

The stink from the cloud of black exhaust was getting to
be too much. Anna caught the eye of the driver and
coughed. He lifted his pinky and twirled his mustache. She
swung her head the other way. She'd leave the line this
minute if it wouldn't mean losing their places—pressed as
they were against a wooden fence with hundreds of other
people waiting to get inside to see the show.

"Stop looking at him like that," Gert said, poking Anna
in the side.

"Like what?"

"With your glamor-girl look," Gert said.

"You're crazy," Anna said.

"You just tossed your hair. Someday you won't get away
with that. Men used to follow you home from the subway for
that look. So don't act so innocent. That look of yours
fooled Abram into marrying you, and then you made him
beg for love all his life."

"You're crazy," Anna said, and then a rock of fear crept
into her mind. "What do you mean?"

"Nothing," Gert said. She adjusted her eyeglasses on
their fake pearl chain. "You know—if it hadn't been for me
Abram never would have had his rightful rewards . . ."

"What rightful rewards?"

"You know what I mean, his wedding night rights."

Anna felt a momentary dizziness. Gert *was* crazy. The
fumes were whirling around her head—she swayed and
leaned back against the wall of the building.

"What's the matter?"

"It's that stink."

"Cover your nose right away with your handkerchief,
Anna. Norman Cousins breathed in fumes from an airplane
and he got a fatal disease."

"It wasn't fatal," Anna corrected her. "He cured it by
laughing at old movies."

"If *you* got it, it would be fatal," Gert warned her. "You
never laugh at low humor, so don't imagine you could start

now. I remember when you were a girl you got nauseous
from Groucho Marx, from Jack Benny, even from Eddie
Cantor. So cover your nose."

"It's impossible that I got nauseous from Groucho Marx,"
Anna said. ". . . and the word is *nauseated*. I never could
bear him, the man disgusted me."

"Exactly," Gert agreed. "You were always too good for
everything."

"Why do you make things up?" Anna demanded. "You're
always telling me things from the old days that never happened."

182   "They happened," Gert said. "It's just convenient for
you not to remember."

"I never tell *you* ridiculous things about yourself!" Anna
said.

"That's right—you never paid attention to me, you never
gave me a thought. You were too busy looking in the mirror,
combing your crowning glory."

"I thought it was Ava who never paid attention to you."

"She's another sister for the books. When it comes to
sisters God wasn't good to me. I always wished we could be
like the Andrews Sisters. But at least I don't have to deal
with Ava now—let her stay in Miami Beach till the cows
come home."

"Let's not get into how much you hate Ava," Anna said,
"or I'll be sorry I invited you along."

"I'm sorry I came already," Gert said.

The truck blurped three shots of black smoke into the air
and tooted its horn. Anna looked up. The driver leaned
forward toward the windshield and made a fish-mouth kiss
at Anna as he pulled away from the curb.

"Disgusting," Gert said as they watched his tail end
merge into traffic. "The world is a sewer these days. Whatever happened to parties and wholesome hayrides?"

"Hayrides!" Anna echoed.

"You can be sure what kind of guest Donahue's having on
today," Gert went on.

"What kind?" Anna asked.

"A sex guest," Gert said. "Donahue always has sex on his show."

"I thought you never watch Donahue."

"I click by him fast on the dial."

"Look," Anna said, "since sex is a fact of life, since you're a woman who's had two husbands by now, why can't you finally face it? If you paid a little attention to what's going on in the world these days, you might come out of the fog of the old days and learn something."

"You should talk! You're the one who doesn't have any understanding of these things. You don't have animal appetites, Anna. You were born with some kind of cotton stuffing inside you instead of flesh."

"*I* was! What about you, the famous virgin at thirty-nine?"

"You weren't a virgin on your wedding night?"

"Of course I was. But I was young! I was still a girl!"

"I know some girls who aren't virgins," Gert said ominously.

"Who?"

"Your granddaughters," Gert said.

"What have *they* got to do with anything? What do you know about them anyway? They don't tell me about their private lives! I'm sure they don't tell *you!* They probably don't even tell their mother!"

"They're college girls," Gert said, "and I know what college girls are up to these days. They live in co-ed dorms. They share the same bathrooms with men!"

"You know everything, don't you?" Anna said in disgust. "If you listened to Donahue like I do, you'd be more understanding of the way the world is today. You could learn something."

"I've watched enough to know exactly what I would learn! I could learn how to be a lesbian and have a baby with my lesbian lover's brother, so we can all be one big happy family."

183

"Oh, get your head out of the Middle Ages," Anna said in disgust. "This is almost the year 2000."

"I'm glad Papa didn't live long enough to see what's become of the world."

"You think Papa was so innocent?" Anna said. "When he married Mama, what do you think he was marrying? Her brains?"

"Bite your tongue," Gert said. "Papa was a religious man."

"He was a *man*," Anna said.

"So was Abram a man," Gert said. "Or didn't you ever notice? You think Abram only wanted to pray on his wedding night?"

184

Anna tried to remember her wedding night. Could such a thing be possible—for a woman to forget her wedding night? "Thank heaven—" she said, "this line is beginning to move." She gave Gert a little shove. "Will you walk?" she said impatiently. "I want to get in there before they fill up."

The line suddenly began to shoot forward. A young woman carrying a walkie-talkie and wearing an NBC peacock emblem on her jacket pocket ran along beside them and herded them into a vast ceilingless cavern. It was like the dark inside of a refrigerator. She rushed them over cables and wires taped to the floor, she sent them up wide flat stairs to find seats.

"Be sure to take an aisle seat," Gert advised Anna, "or he won't be able to get to you."

"What makes you think I care if he gets to me?" Anna asked.

"Because you always have to be the center of attention," Gert said. "But don't bother to toss your hair for him," Gert added. "Your charms had their day, Anna, but face it—their day is over."

Donahue's guest was a young woman who looked like a school teacher but was really a whorehouse madam. Her ancestors had come over on the Mayflower. She was dressed like a girl going to church. Pretty, blonde, and blue-eyed, she sat on a chair and folded her hands in her lap. Her dress resembled a kind of middy-blouse Anna used to wear as a child. A string of white pearls lay on her throat. Anna observed how respectful Phil Donahue was to her; she disapproved. Why should a man as educated and intelligent as Donahue have to knock himself out for a woman like that—running around the audience with his coattails flying and his microphone sticking forward like a giant mushroom.

They were talking about the madam's business—how her "girls" were very smart and cultured, that many were college students, one was even a medical student. What other jobs could they find, she said, that had such good hours and such high pay? She provided regular medical care for them. Her girls carried little charge-card machines in their purses. They carried extra pantyhose and business clothes for the next day. They were refined, intelligent women, just women earning a decent living.

The floodlights, burning brightly now and heating up the room rapidly, seemed aimed at Anna's face. She squinted in the glare. Donahue went on smiling and nodding as if the whorehouse business was just fine with him; the trouble with liberals was that they forgave everyone for everything.

Gert poked Anna.

"Does anyone know what kind of part-time jobs your granddaughters have at college?" she demanded. "Do you think Janet knows what her children do?"

"You're crazy," Anna said. "My granddaughters are not prostitutes."

"Do you know for sure where they sleep every night?"

"No!" Anna said. "Do you know for sure where *I* sleep every night?"

"I have no doubts about you," Gert said. "You aren't the type to sleep around. You only like to tease."

Anna was feeling dizzy. She was the older sister, she had
always believed she understood everything better than
Gert. Now her head was reeling. All these questions raised
about her granddaughters, about her wedding night! Was
she a tease because she liked to wear her skirts short? She
had always had pretty legs, why shouldn't she? She saw in
her mind the red truck, the spurting black smoke, the
truckdriver throwing her a kiss.

"Let's leave," Anna said. "This show is worthless."

"I'm more than willing," Gert said. "For this I had to
waste a taxi coupon."

186   "Look," Anna said, "Donahue could have had on Ralph
Nader talking about poison in hair dye. He could have had
on someone from the PLO. He didn't send me a program.
He's only in LA for a week and this is what we got."

"We got sewage! From the sewer of the world!" Gert said.
She waved her arm to dismiss the whole thing, and suddenly Donahue came bounding up the steps with his microphone quivering in front of him and grabbed Gert's arm.
He leaned right across Anna. He was so close she could see
the thin white stripes on his pinstripe suit, the glare of the
spotlights on his wedding ring. The hairs on his hand
holding the microphone were glowing like hot electric wires.

"C'mon, help me out here!" he said to Gert as he thrust
the black knob toward her mouth, bending toward her as if
he cared with all his heart exactly what Gert thought about
every issue in life. He took her hand and pulled her gently
to a standing position. "Tell us what you think." He had a
voice like a lover.

"What I think," Gert said, "is with all the troubles in the
world, who needs to put a woman like this on national
television!"

A round of applause rose up all around them. The Mayflower Madam smiled sweetly and cast her eyes down; the
applause for Gert was deafening. Donahue smiled at Gert
and squeezed her hand. Anna could smell his cologne or his

aftershave or something from his beautiful white hair. She was the one who had got the free tickets, and Gert was the one who had got to air her small-mindedness all over the United States of America.

Anna raised her hand, but Donahue's back was to her, he was rushing down the stairs—her chance was lost forever. She turned to Gert and saw how flushed her cheeks were. A smile as big as a freeway was on her face.

"He's a real *mensch*," Gert said. "I could go for him."

"I thought he was too liberal for you."

"He's only that way on television. In real life he's married to a good Catholic girl," Gert said. "He knows what's right. **187** He's a good family man. I would be happy for my daughters to marry a man like that."

"You have no daughters," Anna said. "You have no children, and it's lucky for them you don't."

"I wonder if my friends in New Jersey saw me," Gert said as they waited at the curb for a taxi. She had insisted on staying till the very end of the show, and then rushed to join the crush of women as they filed forward to shake Donahue's hand.

"No doubt they saw you all over the continent. Probably the President of the United States heard you, too."

"I hope so. He would agree with my opinion," Gert said. "He and I have the same politics."

"What do you know about politics?" Anna said. "All you ever read is 'Dear Abby.'"

"I know the world used to be a better place. That's all I need to know."

"Oh!" Anna said. *"Why don't you grow up?"*

"You think it's grown up to cry for an hour in the bathroom on your wedding night?" Gert said. "Sitting on the tile in a brown silk dress and bawling your head off?"

"That's nonsense," Anna said. "I never cry. I didn't cry then and I don't cry now."

"You were afraid to be left alone for the night with Abram."

"Not true."

"He came to me and begged me to calm you down. He had a hotel room reserved in Atlantic City, but you didn't want to go away from home after the ceremony. You were hysterical."

"Ridiculous."

"He thought maybe I could arrange it so you and he could spend the first night alone at our house, then you wouldn't be so scared. What I had to go through!"

188 "What did you have to go through?" Anna asked. She couldn't remember a single thing about her wedding except the violent odor of her corsage of gardenias, curling brown at the edges almost as soon as she got them.

"First I had to get Mama farmed out. The Bronx relatives finally agreed to take her home with them and bring her back the next day. Then I had to find a place for myself. Do you know where I had to sleep on your wedding night?"

"No," Anna said coldly. "The way you adored Abram, maybe it was with him. How should I know what else you're making up in this crazy story?"

"He really should have married me," Gert said. "I have a sweeter nature than you. He would have had a better life with me. The fact is, Rosie Dubin and her husband had just taken an apartment on Ocean Parkway, and they agreed to let me come and sleep there after the ceremony. But they had only one double bed. So I had to sleep in it with them. They made me get in the middle, between them, to prove there wouldn't be any hanky-panky to embarrass me."

"It must have been a big night for you, the famous virgin, sleeping in a bed with a man."

"We laughed all night," Gert said, smiling. A big bus blasted past them, and her hair blew back in the wind. She looked almost young and pretty.

"Late as I married, I always enjoyed sex, Anna. Did you?"

"When Donahue has me on as his guest, I'll discuss it in public, not before."

The taxi they'd ordered pulled up, and Gert held the door open as Anna got in. As hard as Anna tried, she could not remember her wedding, her wedding night, her honeymoon. Had she ever enjoyed sex? What a question. She could hardly remember sex. When it happened, it was in the dark, late at night, she was always tired, she kept her eyes closed. Abram never stayed there long, he didn't bother her too often. What was to enjoy? Did Gert know something she didn't know? Did her granddaughters? All her life she had considered herself so advanced, but could it be she was the one still in the Dark Ages?

189

The taxi driver, a handsome Armenian, drove them toward home. He had some music playing on the radio with a low, hard beat. He seemed to be in another world. On Santa Monica Boulevard they passed a porno movie. They passed young girls strutting about in short shorts. They saw two gay men looking in the window of an underwear store, their arms around each other's waists. They passed a billboard with a half-naked woman in a bikini, advertising an airline. Gert had a satisfied expression on her face. Anna suddenly grabbed her arm. "I slept in the same bed with Abram thirty-one years, Gert. I had two babies. Doesn't that prove something to you?"

"What does it prove? Who knows which way you were facing?" She took a red lipstick out of her purse and rolled it around her lips without looking in a mirror. She squeezed her lips together. "You know, I had two husbands already," Gert said. "If this one doesn't hold out, I'll find another one. If necessary, I'll have three, maybe four."

"You're seventy-six years old," Anna said. "You must be crazy."

"So I'm crazy," Gert said. "You should be so crazy. Here, put on some nice bright lipstick and enjoy your life a little, Anna."

THE NEXT MEAL
IS *LUNCH*
. . . .

One of the gay boys across the alley was hucking and hocking in his bathroom, which looked directly into Anna's kitchen window. She pushed away her dish of cottage cheese—how could a person be expected to eat when these poor boys were dying like flies all over the place? And where were their mothers on a special day like this? If one of her daughters had AIDS, Anna would be right there, holding the bowl for her to throw up in, especially on Thanksgiving, when no one should be alone.

She was alone. Accidentally, of course. A big dinner had been planned, as usual, at her daughter Janet's, with Carol making the stuffing and Gert and Harry bringing the canned sweet potatoes. But then Janet had come down with the flu. Anna certainly hoped it was the flu, but these days who could know? She had always thought her son-in-law was perfectly respectable, but from the talk shows Anna knew that almost anyone you met could be a closet bisexual or have a file cabinet full of heroin.

Today was a hard day to be alone. It happened Anna's birthday came this year on Thanksgiving Day, and this one was not chicken feed, this was eighty, this was the Big Time. She'd already been planning how she would break up and distribute the chocolate turkey her daughters always gave her. The hollow head, she'd decided, would go to her youngest granddaughter, who had won a ten-thousand-dollar scholarship to college and proved to Anna—not that she needed proof—the superiority of her genes.

She heard the sick boy cough again, half-choking, half-strangling. Could the AIDS virus leap across an alley? On the news they talked all the time about safe sex! When was sex ever safe? At its best it gave you children, and some children (of course not hers!) could ruin your life as fast as any fatal disease. Thank God Anna was past *that* minefield—no chance of getting pregnant and no chance of having rotten children. Now all she had to worry about was the diseases of old age. When she went, she wanted to go fast. And if she had the bad luck to linger, she only hoped someone would make short work of her.

It crossed her mind she should cook chicken soup for the gay boy and bring it in to him, but, as usual, whenever she had a generous impulse, her good sense ruled it out. Neither did she want to hang around here and listen to him *krekhts* all day.

"So I'm going for a walk," she announced to her furniture, to her two pianos, to the ghosts who hopped around her apartment. "I should only live to see you again, I shouldn't be mugged." This was said to protect her from the evil eye though Anna had no use for those old and meaningless superstitions. Still, if a person anticipated all the terrible conclusions, they couldn't sneak up on you. She didn't take a purse—a strategy designed to discourage muggers, and she took her ID in her sweater pocket, in case she got hit by a truck.

A truck hit Anna the minute she stepped off the curb at Melrose and Fairfax. For the first time in her life she flew like a bird, but grunting. And hit down like a rock, but bursting. Blood was in her mouth. She saw a Mexican jump out of the truck and felt him take her gently under the arms and drag her back on the sidewalk. She was sorry she had ever wished they would all go back to Mexico. He was

192

staring into her eyes with a passion she couldn't identify, but it moved her. She wished he were her son. Daughters could be devious (she was lucky hers were not!) while sons usually adored their mothers. She was about to ask him if he was good to his mother when he stamped his foot.

"Lady! You crazy? You must be blind!" He pinched her arm. "Give me *money*. You make me late for work!"

He growled over her with a dog's mouth, menacing her, his mustache curved like a scythe. Anna felt a veil descend over her eyes.

"Shit, man," he said. "Shit, you losing me my job, man." He kicked at her thigh. She saw him climb back into his truck and roar away. **193**

"Give me money," she mumbled as she lowered her head down to the pavement. "Give me money. That's all anyone knows these days."

THE DAY IS *THURSDAY*
THE CITY IS *NECTAR HILL*
THE WEATHER IS *CLOUDY*
THE NEXT MEAL IS *LUNCH*

The sign hung on the wall directly in front of Anna's bed. Anna privately added a fifth line:

THE PERSON FORCED TO READ THIS IS A *MORON.*

She had lain here during the risings and settings of several suns, but the day remained Thursday, the next meal always lunch. She was strapped into her bed; at intervals she was turned like a frankfurter on a barbecue grill. A pattern of motion occurred around her: white-coated forms circled in the hall. Nurses slid along on their rubber shoes, carrying Dixie cups filled with little pills; aides, with their sullen faces, threw down lunchtrays, refilled water pitchers. An old woman in a red furry robe pushed her wheel-

chair up and down the corridor, crying: "They poison my
food. My son stole my house. What comes out in the toilet is
black. No one believes me." In the background an old man
crooned, "Nonno, nonno," never stopping, never changing
his tone.

The moment Anna's daughters materialized at her bedside, she said, "Get me out of here." She saw them look at
one another. "Listen," she said. "The weather isn't cloudy,
the next meal isn't lunch, and I'm not a vegetable. Not yet."
She motioned to the other two beds in her room, sporting
horrors she preferred not to memorize. "You can't get lox
and bagels here. What does it cost me to stay here a day?"

194

Her girls gave each other another look. They'd already
explained to Anna that the hospital to which the ambulance
had taken her refused to keep her because she wasn't badly
hurt, so until her dizziness went away she had to stay here
in this nursing home. She'd told them she wasn't dizzier
than usual and she wasn't ready for a nursing home. Now a
panic rose in her lower belly, along with a premonition of
her future here, a place from which she couldn't call her
congressman, or write a letter to the newspaper, or threaten
anyone with a lawsuit. Unable to escape, she would be
reduced to a lump of nothing.

She thought of her miserable apartment with longing; it
now seemed as spacious and fragrant as Yosemite itself, her
narrow stall shower a waterfall, her white stove vent a snow-
capped mountain. Never mind the Armenians' barbecue
fumes, never mind the germs coming across the alley from
the gay boy. A haven of freedom was what her apartment
was—where no one told her what day, what weather, what
town she was forced to endure in. Was it possible she would
never get back there?

In a drawer by her bed at home she had her Hemlock
Society card; if her daughters didn't get her out of here, she
would phone the society and ask for the name of some

doctor in Holland who could mail her the correct pills as soon as possible. Was it a major problem that her children would be insulted when they realized they weren't important enough to keep her alive? She began to compose a note to them: *"Believe me, children, this has nothing to do with the way you treated me and it's not that life wasn't worth living, especially with your father (I wish I believed I would meet him and be his footstool in heaven, but dead in my opinion is dead, what can I tell you?) and it's not that my grandchildren aren't dear to me, but look, let's face it, they're not interested in me—do they ever come to visit?"* This last she decided to leave out—she didn't need to create any extra hostility. *Please be advised I'm no coward— you'll find out some day that old age isn't for sissies.*

She began to imagine her funeral: what she wanted was for the girls to play a tape of herself performing Mozart on the piano; maybe a little Chopin, a page or two of the "Pathétique," a little "Claire de Lune"—a sampling of her well-rounded repertoire. Maybe even "The You and I Waltz," the first piece she had ever learned by heart.

But definitely no fancy ceremonies. Certainly no rabbis, those crooks. No strangers either, just a tasteful gathering to the tune of great music, played by Anna's gifted but deceased fingers.

She sensed a breeze passing over her face and saw some papers flutter in front of her eyes.

"Ma?" she heard. She blinked.

"Janet and I have some papers we think you should sign." A thin tube—a pen—was slid into her hand, a hard surface appeared beneath her forearm. They unstrapped her straps.

"What papers?" she said.

"We think you need to let us handle your money from now on, Ma," Janet said. "If you give us your money—then after two years the government will pay for your bills here."

195

"Two years?" Anna yelled. "You think I'm going to stay in this zoo for two years? You're crazy!"

"A lawyer advised us to do this, Ma. It's perfectly legal. It's just a protection."

"You're seeing lawyers about my money?" Anna said. "Who are you protecting?"

She knew the look they were giving each other, it was the look you give over the head of a crazy person.

"What're you doing, Ma?"

Anna rolled out of bed and landed with a clunk on the floor. The stroke victim in the next bed peered down at her and began to hum.

"Listen," Anna said, on her hands and knees, "a Brownie troop is coming tomorrow to bring candy canes. The aides are putting up a Christmas tree in the hall. A chaplain is coming to pray with us and remind us of the suffering of Jesus. You want me to be here for *that?* I'm still your mother, children," she said fiercely, "so get me out of this joint right now."

At Carol's house they argued with her all night. They wanted her to give up her apartment. The time had come. All right, she was a reasonable woman. She could see the sense of some of their arguments: it was dangerous to live alone, hard to shop, she never liked to cook much anyway. In a retirement home she'd have better nourishment, security, care, protection, and, if she fell, help on the spot. The two of them would take care of everything, move her to a place nearby, they'd visit her all the time. (No one said anything about her living with them, but, fine, she was a modern old woman, she knew children didn't take you in anymore.)

"You wouldn't have to visit me all the time, believe me."

"So you'll agree to move?"

"I'm helpless in the hands of fate," Anna said. What can I do?"

196

She moved her two pianos with her; it wasn't easy fitting them into her room, but Anna was gratified to see it made quite an impression on the staff of the Country Gardens Retirement Home, how their mouths dropped open when the elevator groaned under the weight of her instruments, one baby grand, one upright. In her room, she directed the movers to set her bed between the two of them so that she could reach up with either hand and find a keyboard waiting for her.

"So children: this is the last stop," she said lugubriously for her daughters' benefit as the three of them signed registration papers at the desk in the lobby, but she was noticing a bunch of old ladies watching her, ladies with legs like elephants, ladies with eyeglasses like Pyrex plates. She saw a couple of old men, too; nothing to get excited about, stooped over, with walkers, with canes, but she had a feeling it wasn't going to be so bad as she thought. Who knew what energy she still had in her? When had she last had a chance to try out her popularity?

At the end of her first week, one of the old ladies got hold of Anna and said, "Unkind things are being said about you in the dining hall, my dear. Bend lower and I'll tell you." They were examining the menu for the week, tacked on the bulletin board.

"I might slip a disc if I bend down," Anna said. She was very careful now, with the threat of the nursing home in her mind. "Just talk louder."

"You've *got* to wear your skirts longer," the woman whispered to her. "I'm telling you this for your own good. It isn't your fault you have such pretty legs."

"What should I do, cut them off?" Anna asked. The menu in front of them was unbelievable: crab quiche, Louisiana frogs' legs, chimichanga, chile relleno. At moments like this, Anna wished she had not dismissed so viciously the Jewish Home for the Aged. There at least they would occasionally have potato latkes, blintzes, kreplach.

"Also, certain people have noticed, I won't say who, that you don't wear earrings. You don't curl your hair."

"So tell them not to look," Anna said. "Tell them I believe in natural beauty."

"And one more thing we think you should know: stay away from the man in the brown plaid shirt. He has only one thing on his mind—sex."

"Believe me," Anna said, "I wouldn't go near the King of England if he had sex on his mind."

198

The joke going around was that everyone at Country Gardens had AIDS; "Guess what kind of AIDS I have?" "You have AIDS?" "Yeah—hearing aids." Or: "Guess what disease I have?" "What disease?" "Oldtimer's Disease." If it made them happy to be comedians, let them be comedians, like the old lady who came down to dinner one night wearing a Groucho Marx nose. Anna hadn't liked vulgarity as a young woman, and she didn't like it now. Thank heaven she hadn't got coarse with age. Mozart and Culture were her creeds—she'd tell the old ladies to put that in their pipes and smoke it the next time someone asked her what church she attended on Sundays. Or she'd answer that her religion was Beauty, that she got spiritual insights from Rachmaninoff. What else could she say to all those clanking pearl earrings hanging between scrolls of blue-white hair and flowered polyester dresses; how did you defend against a little army of Church Ladies?

Anna wore what was left in her closet from the old days— graceful pleated skirts, sheer stockings, high heels (these she had to wear because of a spur on her instep), and a tailored blouse with a roadrunner pin (a gift from Abram) on the collar. She weighed a hundred pounds; the other old ladies weighed two hundred. She saw them looking at her calves, at her short skirts, and she swung her hips more grandly as she walked down the carpeted halls.

The shape of Anna's days had changed—at home she had had no structure: a walk to Fairfax was her outing, or she could lie there all day like a dog. But here they had everything: an exercycle room (a nurse right next-door), a beauty shop, a library, a crafts room, a bingo room, a banking room where once a week you could cash checks. A maid came and gave you clean towels and sheets. How could she afford this? The fact was she had no money at all anymore; her girls had stripped her of every cent in the interest of some future good. They were paying her bills, and they told her to put money worries out of her mind. If she couldn't trust her children, who could she trust? Her life of responsibility was over. She was free as a bird.

199

Coming toward the dining hall she smelled the luscious odor of frying onions (the thought of onions alone used to make her sick; now her mouth watered). She felt as if this were the college she had never attended, the dormitory life she had never had. Heads turned when she came into the dining hall; if she could still see to thread a needle, she'd sew the hems on all her skirts and make them even shorter.

Of course, when her daughters called her, she complained; the food was awful, the heater didn't work, there were roaches in the bathroom—and when they came to visit, she let her knees buckle, she told them she had headaches, that her sciatica was back, her osteoporosis was going wild. The instant they were gone, she went downstairs and climbed on the exercycle and did a mile.

The man in the brown plaid shirt took a seat across from her at dinner. "I'm Harvey and I'm eighty-six," he said. "I understand you have two pianos. Fancy that. I have two cellos."

"I don't do duets," Anna said.

"I can see you're a smart cookie," he said. "I can see

you've been around. Now me," he said, "I am a famous
architect. I built 280 houses in the San Gabriel Hills alone.
I can prove it." He reached into his pocket and handed her
a photocopy of an article, telling how famous he was.

"I'm not impressed," Anna said, handing it back. "At this
point in my life, only Arthur Rubinstein could impress
me."

"I have it over him," the man said. "I'm still alive."

"Maybe, but only barely," Anna observed. She ordered
her dinner from the waitress. "Easy on the onions," she
said. "I might have a date later on."

200   That night Harvey-plaid-shirt knocked on the door of
her room. When she opened the door, he pulled a gun on
her.

"Stick 'em up," he said. Then he pulled the trigger. A flag
that said "BANG!" fell from the barrel.

"They told me you were a sex maniac," Anna said. "You
go around armed, too?"

"Only when I meet my match," he said. "And I think I
have, kid, with you."

"You certainly are conceited," Anna told him.

"See what I mean?" he said. "I met my match. You and I
are a pair, kid. We're survivors. You don't get to our age
unless you're smart, tough, and lucky."

Just then the phone rang. Anna's sister Gert said: "How
come you weren't in your room last night?"

"I had Bingo."

"A gambler you're becoming in your old age?"

"Don't worry," Anna said. "I use plenty of self-control."

"And the night before?" Gert asked.

"I was at Potpourri. We have an entertainment night. I
was playing the piano for my friends."

"What's this with the nightlife?" Gert asked. "And what
kind of friends? You never made a friend in your life."

"You sound a little jealous," Anna said. "Someday, after
Harry dies, you can move in here. You'll see for yourself."

"Don't tell me you like it there!"

Harvey was aiming his gun at her again.

"Don't aim for the eyes," she warned him.

"You have someone there?" Gert asked.

"A friend, he just stopped by for a minute."

"A man in your room already! And you sound cheerful," Gert accused her. "A week ago you told me this is the last stop!" Gert said. "In your own words you said so. 'I hope I die in my sleep,' you said."

"Now I see it could be a long last stop," Anna said. "It could be a vacation."

Harvey fired his pistol.

201

Anna laughed. She had the clear impression she was getting younger.

S   9329

AUTHOR   Gerber

TITLE   Chattering man

DATE DUE	BORROWER'S NAME

OCT
OCT 2
NOV
JAN

S   9329

Gerber
Chattering man